Natalie's dress slid to the floor. She was wearing nothing beneath it.

Chance gripped her shoulders hard. "I want to know who the hell you are."

Natalie smiled and stepped toward him. "I can be anyone you want."

He couldn't wait any longer to touch her. Clamping one arm around her waist, he pulled her into the shower with him.

She grabbed the soap playfully. "I can be Rachel." Her slick hands slid over his skin, leaving trails of ice and fire in their wake. Her fingers drew a line to his waist and then lower. He closed his eyes as her hot fist enclosed him.

"Or I can be Calli." She began to stroke him gently.

"Or I can be both." Her laugh was a breath in his ear before her tongue darted inside. "I could be two women at once. Is that what you want?"

All Chance was certain of was that he needed her with a desperation that threatened to slice him in two. "What I *want* is *you. Now.*"

Blaze™

Dear Reader,

D.C. cop Natalie Gibbs prides herself on being able to handle men on the job and off…until Chance Mitchell comes into her life and she finds she wants her hands on the sexy insurance investigator a bit too much. When Chance proposes one night of no-strings, no-complications, no-etiquette sex, the very practical Natalie sees his proposition as the perfect way to get him out of her system for good.

The problem is that one night with Chance Mitchell isn't nearly enough, and after three months Natalie decides that she's willing to run any risk to lure him back into her bed—even if she has to disguise herself to do it….

This is just the beginning of Natalie and Chance's adventure. I hope you'll come along for the ride and watch them ultimately take the biggest risk any two people can take when they risk their hearts.

Developing this miniseries—RISKING IT ALL—has allowed me to write about three fascinating triplet sisters who have very different dreams, talents and goals. But they have one thing in common—they're willing to risk everything to get what they want. I hope you will look for Rory's and Sierra's stories, *The Dare* (June) and *The Favor* (July), and that you will enjoy reading them as much as I have enjoyed writing them.

I would love to hear what you think about these stories. You can e-mail me through my Web site, www.carasummers.com.

Happy reading!

Cara Summers

THE
PROPOSITION
CARA
SUMMERS

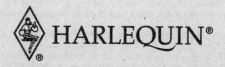

HARLEQUIN®

TORONTO • NEW YORK • LONDON
AMSTERDAM • PARIS • SYDNEY • HAMBURG
STOCKHOLM • ATHENS • TOKYO • MILAN • MADRID
PRAGUE • WARSAW • BUDAPEST • AUCKLAND

To my sister in heart and dear friend—Kathy Eagan.
Thanks for your support, your inspiration and your
never-wavering belief in me. I love you.
And to all sisters everywhere.

ISBN 0-373-79188-7

THE PROPOSITION

Printed in U.S.A.

Prologue

Summer 1999

HARRY GIBBS was a man who'd spent his life taking risks and loving every minute of it. For an international jewel thief, risks were a part of the game, and Harry had always played the game very well.

Of course, he'd been born smart and lucky. As for his other talents—such as his Houdini-like knack for opening locks and his gift for disguise—well, those he'd honed to perfection over the years.

And look where his chosen profession had gotten him. Standing on the balcony of his Tuscan villa, Harry watched as the summer sun bathed the vineyards below in a golden light. Although he had a small cottage outside of Dublin and an apartment in Paris, this was his favorite residence in between jobs.

Some would call his the perfect life.

Harry bit back a sigh. No life was perfect, and he had reason to know this better than most men. Life, he'd discovered, boiled down to a series of choices that you either embraced or rejected. Ten years ago, he'd made a big decision—to leave his wife and ten-year-old triplet daughters behind so that he could resume his career as a master thief.

His wife Amanda had wanted Natalie, Rory and Sierra to have a "normal" life. He'd wanted that for the girls, too. So for ten years, he'd tried, but in the end he just couldn't accept that "normal" life for himself.

As the light pouring over the valley slowly darkened and the shadows lengthened, Harry finally let out the sigh he'd been holding back. There wasn't a day that passed when he didn't miss his family. And on this particular warm summer night, the twentieth anniversary of the day the triplets were born, he missed them more than ever.

He moved into the salon, then crossed to the bar and poured champagne into a flute. Six more years—he and Amanda had agreed on that. He wouldn't contact the girls or try to see them until their twenty-sixth birthday.

Tonight, the six years seemed like forever, and lately he'd begun to feel that perhaps time was running out for him.

He crossed to his desk and opened the photo album to three pictures he'd taken of his oldest daughter, Natalie. Then he raised his glass in a toast.

"To my courageous Natalie," he murmured. "Happy birthday."

In many ways, she was the most like him. Sipping the icy liquid, he continued to study the images arranged on the page. They were his favorites. The first was one he'd taken when she'd had her tonsils out. She'd been twelve, and though she hadn't known, he'd joined Amanda to sit by her side the night she'd spent in the hospital. The second was of Natalie getting her diploma at her high school graduation. That was just one of many days that he'd missed being with his girls.

His agreement with Amanda hadn't stopped him from secretly attending important events in their lives and doing his best to watch them grow up. He just hadn't ever been able to let them know he was there.

When they were small, his girls had idolized him. The last thing Amanda had wanted for them was that they would romanticize the career path he'd chosen. He didn't want that either.

Harry bent to get a closer look at the picture he'd snapped of Natalie during her first day at the police academy. He grinned. No way was his oldest daughter going to follow in his path. If anything, she seemed determined to uphold the laws that he had lived his life breaking.

And that was his Natalie to a *T.* From the time she'd been able to walk and talk, she'd taken on the responsibility of both defending and ensuring just treatment of her sisters. A series of images streamed through his mind. In each of them, Natalie would stand in front of her sisters like a warrior. By the time she was ten, Harry could see that his oldest daughter had inherited not merely his red hair, but also his knack for opening locks and his talent for disguise. She would have made a great jewel thief.

Raising his glass, Harry drank to that. Of his three girls, Natalie had always been the biggest risk-taker, and he couldn't help but wonder if being a cop would help her to come to terms with that side of her nature.

If he could just talk to her…

And what the hell good would that do? Harry set down his glass. What could he say? The problem was he wanted his girls to be able to have their cake and eat it, too—but he and Amanda hadn't found a way to do that.

His gaze shifted to the framed photo of his wife, one he'd snapped at the girls' graduation. Reaching out, he ran a finger down the side of her cheek. He'd never stopped loving her.

And he'd never stopped loving his daughters. Thinking of Natalie, Harry reached for a sheet of paper and a pen and sat down at the desk. His risk-taking daughter, his seekers of justice, wouldn't hesitate to take action. There had to be something he could say to her. Even if he couldn't send the letter now, he'd find a way to get it to her eventually.

Harry took another sip of champagne in a toast to his oldest daughter. And then he began to write.

Dearest Natalie…

1

Spring 2005

CHANCE MITCHELL had never before been obsessed by a woman in his life. He glanced down the table to where Detective Natalie Gibbs was sipping a glass of white wine. He continued to study her as she tucked a stray curl behind her ear. The two women seated next to her could be described as equally attractive, but ever since he'd joined his friends for a celebration at the Blue Pepper, his gaze had returned to Natalie.

At nine o'clock the popular Georgetown bistro was crowded. Customers were lined up three deep at the bar, and a salsa band was playing on the patio. In some corner of his mind, Chance was aware of that, just as he was vaguely aware of the ongoing conversation at his table, but his focus remained on the fascinating detective.

Her hair fell past her shoulders, and in the dim light of the bar, the red-gold curls looked as if they might burst into flames at any moment. He wanted to touch those curls. He wanted to touch her, slowly and thoroughly.

Chance took a long swallow of his beer, but it did little to cool the heat that burned inside of him. Oh, he was obsessing all right, and he wanted to know why.

What he felt for Natalie had begun the first moment he'd seen her. They'd both been working undercover for different agencies, and she'd been disguised when she'd walked into his art gallery. From the instant their eyes had met, there'd been a connection. He'd felt a curious shock of recognition that had registered like a punch in his gut.

So far, he hadn't acted on the attraction. During the three days that he and Natalie had joined forces and worked as partners, the cool, aloof redhead had kept him at arm's length. And he'd let her. That's what he couldn't quite figure out. He was a man who knew how to get what he wanted, but Natalie Gibbs had him hesitating in a way he couldn't recall doing since he'd been a teenager.

Perhaps it was time he put a stop to that. She didn't look quite so cool tonight. Maybe it was the clothes. When they'd worked as partners, she'd always worn a jacket and slacks, the standard uniform of a woman who worked in a man's world. But tonight, the blouse she wore left her arms and throat bare, and the lacy, sheer fabric revealed curves as well as skin.

His eyes shifted to the V-neck that ended just where he imagined the valley between her breasts began. He let his gaze lower to the tiny, pearl buttons that marched in a narrow line to her waist. He could imagine unbuttoning them one at a time, very slowly, drawing out the pleasure for them both.

As the images filled his mind, the tightening in his gut turned raw and primitively sexual. Why in hell was he hesitating? Desire was something he was familiar with. He could handle it. Or he could walk away. Couldn't he?

He took another swallow of his beer.

"You all right?"

Chance tore his gaze away from Natalie to face the two men seated beside him. Tracker McBride had asked the question. But it was Lucas Wainwright who was studying him thoughtfully. Seven years ago, Tracker and Lucas had worked with him in a Special Forces unit, and in the past two weeks, they'd had the opportunity to work together again to crack a smuggling ring operating in D.C. Tonight, they were supposed to be celebrating the successful closure of the case, and this was the second time he'd lost track of the conversation, thanks to Detective Natalie Gibbs.

"I think he has his eye on the fair detective," Lucas said.

Tracker's look turned speculative. "Really?"

Knowing that the best defense was a good offense, Chance said to Tracker, "Have you and Sophie set a date yet?"

Tracker's gaze went to the tall blonde sitting to Natalie's right.

Lucas grinned. "I hear from Mac that Sophie is talking about a fall wedding."

Chance mentally shook his head at the satisfied expression on Tracker's face and shifted his gaze to the third woman who sat at the other end of the table, Dr. MacKenzie Lloyd Wainwright. Mac and Lucas had been married for a year, and they were expecting a child. He'd never envisioned either of his friends marrying and settling down.

"Now that Lucas and I are pretty much spoken for, it's your turn," Tracker said.

Chance held both hands out, palms up. "Not a chance in hell." Then he laughed as his friends winced at the pun. He just wasn't the marrying kind.

It wasn't that he didn't like women. He did. And you could italicize the plural. Not that he had ever involved himself with more than one woman at a time. Going down that particular path had always seemed to him to be way too complicated if not downright suicidal. He'd always made sure that his relationships were simple, uncomplicated and a lot of fun while they lasted. *Permanent* wasn't a word that existed in his vocabulary. Hell, nothing was permanent—not in this life.

"I don't know," Tracker said. "Sophie says that there's a real spark between you and the detective."

The sudden ringing of a phone had all three men reaching for their cells. Whoever was getting the call, Chance figured he was saved by the bell. Lucas opened his and a second later said, "I'm going to have to take this in a quieter spot." Rising, he signaled Tracker to come with him. The two friends worked together now. Lucas ran his family's company, Wainwright Enterprises, and Tracker headed up security for him.

Chance sipped his beer and found his gaze returning to Natalie. When she glanced up and met his eyes, there was a moment, a long moment, when everything else faded. A heated discussion at a nearby table, laughter from the bar, even the low sound of a saxophone became just a buzz in his ears. The faces of the other two women at the table blurred, and all he could see was Natalie.

Twin sensations assaulted him—a hard punch to his gut and a strange flutter just beneath his heart. No, this wasn't the reaction he had to just any woman. Why did this particular woman have this kind of effect on him? A part of him wanted to find out; another part of him wanted to run.

The realization had a spurt of panic moving through him. No woman had ever made him want to run before.

"Hey." Tracker's amused tone only penetrated when he felt the nudge to his shoulder. Turning, Chance discovered that Lucas had moved to help Mac from her chair. "Our party's breaking up," Tracker said. "Mac's tired so they're driving home now. Sophie and I are going to walk back to her place. Do you need Lucas to give you a lift back to your hotel?"

"No," he said as he rose from his chair. It had been years since he'd allowed himself to run away from anything. That part of his life was over. He was flying to London in the morning, but there was one thing he was going to do before he left. Chance moved with Tracker down to the other end of the table.

"Sorry to be such a party pooper," Mac said, stifling a huge yawn.

"I'm the one who yawned first," Sophie said. "The last few days have been hectic." Then she smiled at Natalie. "But you should stay. Chance is an excellent dancer, and the music is good."

"No, I—" Natalie began as she rose from her chair.

"Sophie's right on one point," Chance said. "The music is very good."

"Please. Don't let me break up your evening," Mac said, taking Natalie's hand and squeezing it. "Stay and have at least one dance. If I weren't asleep on my feet,

I'd drag Lucas out. There's nothing more romantic than dancing under the stars."

"What's one dance?" Sophie said softly as she kissed Natalie's cheek.

Chance waited until the two couples had taken their leave. "We don't have to dance if you're afraid of that Latin beat."

Natalie's eyes narrowed as she met his. "I can dance to that if you can."

It was just the reaction Chance had hoped for. The one thing he'd learned from working with the beautiful detective was that she was never afraid to take a risk. That was his key, he realized as he took her hand and led her toward the patio. If he framed his proposition in the right way, they'd be taking a different kind of risk together before the night was over.

NATALIE KNEW she was making a mistake the moment that Chance took her hand. It wasn't that he hadn't touched her before. He was a very physical man. In the brief time they'd worked together, he'd taken her arm, or placed a hand at her back. But he'd never before held her hand. His was hard, his fingers callused, and just the pressure of his palm against hers had little ribbons of heat uncurling up her arm.

The intensity of the sensations had her wondering what it would feel like when he really touched her. And she'd been thinking of that since they'd first met in that art gallery. He'd been a possible suspect in an art theft ring, and it had been her job to keep an eye on him.

Natalie sent him a sideways glance as he made a

path for them through the crowd. Keeping an eye on Chance Mitchell was nice work if you could get it.

He was a man any woman would look twice at. He had a long, rangy body that wore jeans and Armani suits with the same careless ease. Hair that looked brown one minute and blond the next. Eyes that were trapped somewhere between a smoky gray and blue. And a face that wasn't quite handsome until he smiled in a certain way.

But for the three days they'd worked side by side, it was his hands that she'd become obsessed with— hands that held a priceless sculpture or a gun with equal skill. More than once, she'd struggled with fantasies of how those long, clever fingers might pleasure a woman.

And she knew enough about men to know that he was fantasizing just as much as she. The fact that she and Chance had been assigned to protect Sophie Wainwright from a ruthless killer had helped both of them keep their focus. But now…Sophie was safe. The case was over. There was nothing to divert her attention from this man. And she wanted him with an intensity that she'd never felt for anyone else.

Why?

Natalie found part of her answer the moment Chance drew her into his arms. Heat streamed through her and every nerve in her body began to throb. No one had ever made her feel this way, and she knew that this was only a promise of what he could make her feel if she would just let him.

Why was she so hesitant to do that?

"We fit perfectly," he murmured.

Hadn't she known they would? She was tall, but he was taller. His chin brushed her hair, and as he guided her across the small dance floor, his thigh pressed briefly against hers. The shock to her system had her stumbling even more closely against him.

"Relax." His voice was just a breath in her ear as he ran those clever fingers up and then down her spine.

"Just listen to the music and let yourself go."

Let yourself go. Natalie bit back a sigh as she struggled against doing just that. She'd always prided herself on her control where men were concerned. Two years of working on a D.C. police special task force had given her plenty of experience handling males, both on the job and in the bedroom as well. In the two serious relationships she'd had, her lovers had both been intimidated by the fact that she was a cop, and she'd learned from experience not to invest too much of herself in a relationship.

Instinct told her that Chance was different. He'd have the ability to break her control, and the idea of that tempted her almost as much as it made her wary.

When Chance drew back a little, Natalie barely kept herself from protesting.

"Much better," he said. "Relaxation is the key."

Of course, it was easy to relax when her bones were melting. But Natalie kept that to herself. Instead, she made herself focus. "You really do know how to dance. Where did you learn?"

"Here and there. I've found it a very useful tool."

She raised her brows. "Tool?"

Chance smiled at her. "Absolutely. Dancing is the easiest method I know for getting a woman into my arms, and second only to my cooking for getting a woman into my bed."

Bed. She should have had a quick comeback for that. Or at least she could have snorted. But the image, as well as the way he'd leaned close to her ear to say it, had a fresh wave of desire streaming through her.

The rhythm of the dance changed abruptly, and Chance slid his hands to her hips, pulling her close for one brief contact. Heat flashed through her as she felt the long hard length of him. The lower part of her body burned and melted. "Oh, yes," one part of her mind said—even as another part said, "Get away while you can!"

But the negative voice in her mind was losing strength, and Natalie suddenly realized that she wasn't going to play it safe. Hadn't some part of her made that decision when she'd chosen her clothes tonight?

The admission sent a hot erotic thrill moving through her. A sliver of panic followed. It wasn't like her to be thinking this way. Just as it wasn't like her to dress with the intention of tempting a man. As the oldest child—by a few minutes anyway—she'd always been the responsible one, and she'd always had to control that wild, reckless streak inside of her that she'd inherited from her father.

"I want you, Natalie." The words were nothing more than a breath in her ear, but her knees turned to water. She was suddenly aware that he'd steered her off the dance floor and into a darkened corner of the patio. Potted trees surrounded them; a brick wall pressed against her back. And he stood before her, the heat of his body so close…

"I want to take you to bed, I want to touch you—all over."

She couldn't prevent the quick thrill the words brought her any more than she could prevent her heart from beginning to hammer.

"I—"

"No." He pressed a finger against her lips. "Let me finish. I have a proposition for you. I'm flying to London tomorrow morning. If I'm lucky, the assignment will take three months. If not, I'll be gone even longer. So there's just tonight." He drew his finger down that line of her throat to the vee of her blouse and then down the tiny pearl buttons one by one. She was sure that her heart skipped a beat at each one.

"Spend just one night with me," he said.

SHE HAD TO SAY YES, Chance told himself. He'd chosen his words very carefully. He always did where women were concerned. One night with no strings was just the kind of proposition that the cool, logical Natalie Gibbs he'd come to know would find irresistible. He figured she was cautious when it came to men because she didn't want complications.

But as he stared into those cool, green eyes, he couldn't get a hint of what she was thinking. She had to have felt at least part of what he'd experienced when they'd been dancing—the incredible promise of what they could share. And she had to be experiencing at least some of the desperation that he was feeling right now.

When he saw her lips part to speak, he raised his fingers to rest them there. "Don't say no. I—" Chance broke off the moment that he realized what had nearly slipped out of his mouth. He'd almost said, "I need you." And that wasn't true. Being a little obsessed was one thing, but need?

Taking a quick breath, he spoke around the bubble of panic that had risen into his throat. "Just think about it. When was the last time you had sex for the sheer fun of it—no strings, no complications? No worrying about the morning-after etiquette? C'mon. What do you say?"

For a moment his question hung in the air between them. One night with Natalie Gibbs—that was what he wanted. And he wanted it very badly. That was all. Need had nothing to do with it. Chance Mitchell hadn't needed anyone for a very long time.

Natalie took his fingers and removed them from her mouth. "That's your proposition? No-strings, no-complications, no-etiquette sex?"

"Exactly." Chance made himself stop with one word. Because he was very much afraid that he was going to babble. Worse still, he just might beg.

Her grin was quick and wicked. He'd never seen that look on her face before, and his heart did a little stutter.

"Proposition accepted," she said.

Chance's heart stopped altogether.

NATALIE LED the way down a narrow flagstone path to the back of a Federal-style house just three blocks away from the Blue Pepper. Lantern lights hung on either side of the door to her apartment.

She'd never before brought a man here—to her own space. But when Chance had suggested her place because it had to be closer than his hotel on Sixteenth Street, Natalie hadn't argued. If she was going to give herself over to one night of reckless, no-strings, no-etiquette sex, she might as well do it in familiar surroundings.

Chance had said nothing since they'd left the Blue Pepper. He hadn't touched her either, but she'd been very much aware of him walking at her side. When she drew the key out of her purse and slid it into the door, he laid a hand on hers.

She turned to look at him then. The full moon poured brightly into the garden behind him, but Chance's face was caught in shifting shadows. His eyes were dark, and she couldn't read what he was thinking.

"Second thoughts?" he asked.

The kindness of the question had some of the nerves in her stomach settling. But she'd made her decision, and she wasn't going to run away from it. Shaking her head, she said, "You?"

"No."

She led the way into the narrow foyer. After shutting the door with his foot, Chance moved quickly, using his arms and body to cage her against the wall.

"It's not a night for any kind of thought," he murmured as he lowered his mouth to within a breath of hers. "Tonight we're just going to feel."

Any lingering doubts streamed away in that first touch of his lips to hers. His mouth was firm, but giving, his hands almost gentle as he ran them up her arms and slipped them into her hair. And his taste—there was a dark sweetness there that she hadn't expected.

Natalie had one long moment to take a heady sample of it before he moved in even closer. His body, rock-hard, pressed against her, and she felt her own body soften and yield in response. He nipped her bottom lip then slid his tongue over hers.

Heat, one glorious, scorching wave of it, rushed up and over her. If she'd ever been more aware of a man before, she couldn't recall it. Everything about him was hard—his chest, his hands, the angle of his hip and the long length of his thigh. Even his mouth had grown harder, more demanding, as if he was determined to find some flavor that she was hiding from him.

It wasn't sweetness she tasted anymore, but a hungry desperation. Was it his or hers?

And all the while those clever, glorious hands raced over her—tracing the curve of her throat, cupping her breasts, and gripping her bottom to pull her even closer. Fire licked along her nerve endings as one sensation after another pulsed through her. Her body had throbbed before, but not like this. Her heart had hammered before, but not as if it intended to burst right out of her chest.

"More."

Had she said the word aloud? The question had barely formed in her mind, when he answered it by slipping fingers into the vee of her blouse and ripping it open. Then in a lightning move, he jerked what remained of her blouse down her arms, trapping her hands at her sides.

Vulnerability. It was a feeling she'd fought against all of her life. But Natalie welcomed it now, along with the deeply erotic thrill that shot through her. She'd prided herself on always being in charge—on the job, in bed. Now, as those hard hands moved over her again, she couldn't remember why she'd even wanted to be in control. When he began to use his mouth on her, she gave herself over to a fresh storm of sensations—the hot, rough texture of his tongue at her throat, the scrape of his teeth at her shoulder. One instant she burned, the next, she shivered.

Someone laughed. She didn't recognize the low, sultry sound, and then his mouth closed over her breast. Fire, furious flames of it, sped along her nerve endings. There was another rip of cloth as she tore her arms free from her blouse. Then she threaded her fingers through his hair and tried to drag his mouth back to hers.

"More," she repeated.

Her whispered plea became a drumbeat in his mind as hunger and need tangled inside of him. He'd been right that it wasn't a night for thinking. He couldn't seem to grab on to one coherent thought. Nor could he resist returning for one more sample of her mouth.

Would he ever get enough of the sweet, drugging flavor of her surrender, that throaty gasp of pleasure that ended in his name? And her scent—something wild and exotic that made him think of taking her quickly on a deserted, moonlit beach while waves thundered furiously over the sand.

Another second and he would simply drown in her. Drawing back, Chance fought to breathe, to clear his mind.

"Hurry. Please."

Her words started his blood pounding in his head.

Helpless to resist, he covered her lips again with his and plundered. This time it wasn't sweetness he tasted, but a hunger as sharp and desperate as his own. The hands running over him were as eager and determined to possess as his. The change in her from surrender to fevered urgency swamped his senses, and need sliced through him.

His fingers fumbled as he tore her belt free and sent her slacks pooling to the floor. He ran his hand down her, pushing aside the remaining barrier of silk. Hanging on to a thin thread of control, he lifted his head—because he had to see her, needed to see her, as he slipped two fingers into her heat. She locked around him, and he watched her eyes darken and cloud as she absorbed the pleasure he was giving her. He knew the moment her climax began, and when she reached the peak, it was his name she breathed. The sound sliced through him and sharpened an ache deep inside him, sharper than any he'd ever known.

Even as the last ripples of her climax moved through her, Natalie knew she had to have more of him. Of this man. Of Chance. She pulled his shirt free and tugged at his belt. Together, they struggled to free him of slacks, T-shirt, shoes until the only barrier between them was the thin black fabric of his briefs. Unable to take the time to pull them down, she closed her hand over him.

"The bedroom." His voice was ragged.

"Here," she replied.

They dragged each other to the floor. Once they were there, she lost no time. Rolling herself on top of him, she began to explore him with her mouth, using her tongue and teeth on his shoulder, his throat, his chest. She couldn't get enough. Her heart had never beaten this hard. Her body had never ached this sharply.

Rising to her knees, she straddled his thighs, dragged down his briefs. Hands clamped at her waist. He lifted her clear of the floor, and then she was sinking onto him. The moment he filled her, they began to move. Through a haze, she saw his smoky eyes, locked on hers as he filled her, withdrew, then filled her again. Pleasure, waves of it, engulfed her as they both increased the pace. As her vision grayed, she leaned down to cover his mouth with hers.

"Now," she murmured against his lips. "Come with me, now."

In one lightning move, he rolled her beneath him. Then he drove her, drove them both, until together they reached that peak and shattered.

2

Three months later...

WITH ONE HAND, Chance Mitchell reached into the cooler at his side and pulled out a beer. He was being watched. It was nothing that he could see in his brief scan of the shoreline—not yet. Still, the moment the boat he was on had rounded that last curve of the coast, all of Chance's senses had gone on alert.

"The hair on the back of my neck tells me that I'm posing for pictures," Tracker said from his position behind the wheel.

"Yeah," Chance replied. That cinched it. If there was one person whose instincts he trusted more than his own, it was Tracker's. "I'm getting the same feeling."

Chance twisted off the cap on his beer and took a long swallow, all the while keeping a tight grip on his fishing pole. To any observer he looked like he was enjoying the fishing that the waters off the south Florida coast provided. That's exactly what he wanted the security people he knew were watching him to believe.

And if they checked into it—as he was sure they were doing right now—they would find that the boat was registered to Lucas Wainwright III, CEO of Wainwright Enterprises, and that the man himself had indeed flown in from D.C. to spend the weekend in Boca Raton and had had his boat brought in from his place on the Keys.

Chance pulled his hat down hard. Luckily, he and his old friend Lucas were the same height and build, so all he'd had to do was use temporary black dye on his hair. But there was no telling how powerful those cameras were, and he didn't want anyone on shore getting a good look at his facial features.

Something hit the line hard. The pole bent nearly double, then twanged upward. Chance nearly laughed out loud. Sometimes, he really loved undercover work. Here he was, on a job staking out the isolated Florida estate of Carlo Brancotti—a millionaire who'd made his fortune stealing from others—and he was going to have the pleasure of battling and landing a big catch. He couldn't have planned it better for the audience that he was sure was recording his every move.

The only thing that might please him more was to land Carlo himself. Two years ago, a huge yellow diamond, the size of a baby's fist, had disappeared from the Ferrante private collection in Rome, and Chance had been on Brancotti's trail ever since. The theft had occurred while the jewel was in transport between the Ferrante palace and the museum where it was to be displayed. The real diamond had been taken and an amazingly accurate fake had been substituted.

From the moment he'd been called in to investigate the heist, Chance had been sure that Brancotti was the mastermind behind it. He'd been tracking the man for a long time, and Brancotti's trademark was to leave an almost undetectable fake in place of the real jewel. By the time the theft was discovered, Brancotti would have found a buyer, and there would be no evidence to connect the man with the crime.

In this case, the substitution had been discovered within days because Count Ferrante had insisted on an appraisal of the diamond for insurance purposes just before the exhibition was opened to the public.

Chance had sold the insurance company and the count on offering a reward for the diamond, one large enough to tempt Brancotti to give it back. And Brancotti had taken the bait. It had been a good idea. If it had worked, the count would have gotten his diamond back, and Chance would have settled an old score and put Brancotti behind bars.

But the plan had gone terribly wrong, and Chance had lost his partner, Venetia Gaston.

The fish pulled hard on his line, and Chance dragged his thoughts back to the present. Mindful of the telescopic lens he was sure was aimed at him, he began to play the fish, releasing the tension on the line and then gradually pulling it taut again.

For two long years, he'd waited for news of a large yellow diamond to surface, and a week ago it had. Through one of his contacts, he'd received a tip that Carlo Brancotti was inviting a very select group of men and women to a weekend at his retreat in south Florida and that the Ferrante diamond would be auctioned off to the highest bidder.

The heightened security along the shoreline of Carlo's estate cinched it. Carlo Brancotti was meticulously careful. That was why he'd never been caught.

Tilting his head slightly, Chance kept one eye on his pole as he scanned the shoreline. The south Florida sun beat down, sending sparks skimming across the backwash the boat was creating, but he didn't miss the flash in the thick cypress trees that lined the shore, light reflecting off a lens. Someone was definitely watching them. He felt the quick kick of adrenaline that he always experienced when he knew the hunt was about to begin.

"Showtime," he said to Tracker. "I'm going to need your help with this fish. It's big."

"Damn. You have all the luck."

A second later, his old buddy was at his side. He'd been pleased when Tracker had agreed to help him with the case—they made a good team. Together, they watched the fish leap out of the water in a huge, graceful arc. The pole bent nearly double again as the fish dove below the surface.

"You spot anything?" Tracker asked as he grabbed Chance's chair to steady it.

"One of them is at two o'clock as you face the shore."

"Got it," Tracker said. "There's another one about a thousand yards to the left."

The fish cleared the water again.

"A lot of security," Chance remarked as he reeled in the line.

"Must be something needs guarding," Tracker said.

"That's the way I figure it, too. Keep a watch, will you? Landing this fish is going to require all of my attention. And if they're watching me, maybe you can pick out a few more of them."

"Right," Tracker said.

For the next few minutes, they said nothing as Chance let out the line and then drew it in, over and over. By the time Tracker dipped the net over the side of the boat and they hauled the fish in, the boat had moved past the Brancotti estate.

Chance waited until they'd turned and were headed back. Tracker kept the throttle open, and Chance stood at the wheel with him while the video camera on the stern side of the boat recorded every inch of the shoreline. This time there was no telltale flash of light. Evidently, their cover had held. The photos that would make their way to Brancotti would show a very happy fisherman, heading home after a satisfying catch.

"Can you get in along the shore without being detected?" Chance asked.

Tracker grinned. "Is the Pope Catholic?"

"Carlo doesn't leave anything to chance."

"Getting you *off* the estate will be the easy part. You've got the tough job. You've got to get *on* the estate by getting invited to the party. And you have to steal the diamond."

Chance smiled at his old friend. "I've got an invite already, thanks to a contact of mine. As for stealing the diamond—that will be the fun part."

Turning, Tracker studied his friend for a minute. "This is more than a job to you, isn't it?"

"Carlo and I go back a long way." Longer than Chance would ever admit to anyone. He and Carlo had lived in the same orphanage for a year—one long year when he'd been a scrawny twelve-year-old and Carlo had been seventeen and his only friend and mentor. Of course, their names had been different then. Chance had hero-worshipped the older boy. But the friendship had died the night that Carlo had robbed the orphanage and made sure that Chance got the blame for the theft. That had been twenty years ago.

Tracker shot his friend a look. "If it's personal between you and Brancotti, that could get in your way."

"I won't let it."

"Is there any chance he'll recognize you?"

"No. I was twelve the last time we saw each other."

Tracker frowned, then said, "Why don't I go in with you? I could pose as your bodyguard or your personal assistant."

Chance grinned and shook his head. "Thanks, but I already have a partner in mind, and you won't fit into the wardrobe."

"There's a wardrobe?"

"An expensive one. I'll be posing as Steven Bradford. You probably haven't heard of him because he's very low-key, but he's a software genius who made his billions in the high-tech boom. And as Steven, I'll be bringing along my latest companion, a model type who, with my backing, is hoping to jettison her career into supermodel status."

Tracker grinned. "The nerd and his arm candy."

"Exactly." Chance paused, then said what he'd been thinking about ever since he'd accepted the assignment. "I'm going to ask Natalie Gibbs to work with me."

Tracker thought for a minute. "She's a looker all right."

"She's the right body type and with blond hair she'll be a dead ringer for Catherine Weston, who now calls herself 'Calli.'" But it wasn't just her looks that had kept Detective Natalie Gibbs in his mind and in his dreams for three straight months.

"I did some research on her." He'd run a thorough check on Natalie, partly to figure out why she'd gotten to him. "Her father, Harry Gibbs, was an international jewel thief. One of those legends who's the prime suspect in every big heist, but who never got caught. He died in an accident about six years ago."

"The father's a jewel thief and the daughter becomes a cop. Interesting."

Fascinating was the word Chance would have chosen. The hell of it was, the more he'd learned about Natalie Gibbs, the more intrigued by her he'd become. "She's not the only daughter. She's the oldest of a set of triplets." According to one source he'd talked to, Natalie took her position as the oldest quite seriously, especially since their mother had passed away six years ago.

"She evidently inherited some of her father's talents," Chance continued. "She worked her way through college cracking safes for various law enforcement agencies."

Tracker eased the boat around a curve of land that cut them off from the Brancotti estate, then turned to study his friend. "Sophie's pretty sure that there's something going on between the two of you. Or that there could be something. She swears that sparks fly whenever you're in the same room together."

Chance shrugged. "It won't interfere with the job."

"It could interfere with your thinking. Take it from someone who's been there."

"The bottom line is I need her for the job. She's got

a cool head." Except for when she was exploding in his arms. "Plus, she has a gift for disguise and a knack for undercover work."

Tracker hadn't taken his eyes off Chance. "You're sure about this?"

Chance met Tracker's eyes steadily. "She's exactly what I want." That was nothing less than the truth. Even before that one night in her apartment, he'd wanted her more than any other woman he'd ever met. The mistake he'd made was to think that having her once would get her out of his system. His miscalculation about that wasn't the only error he'd made that night. He'd never been so rough with a woman before. Hell, he'd ripped her clothes off and taken her on the floor of her foyer. And he hadn't been much gentler later in her bed.

To top everything off, he'd left before she'd awakened and flown off to London without so much as a note or a phone call to say goodbye. Chance liked women, and he prided himself on treating them well. But he hadn't treated Natalie very well.

Truth be told, his response to Natalie Gibbs had scared him. It hadn't been just the lack of control he'd had over his physical response to her. No. There'd been a moment when he'd stood in the doorway of her bedroom watching her sleep when he simply hadn't wanted to leave. Ever.

That was unprecedented. Chance Mitchell never stayed in one place, never intended to settle down. He changed his name as often as he changed locations. But something about Natalie Gibbs pulled at him. That was why he hadn't called or sent flowers. Now, three months later, he wanted her to help him catch Brancotti. And he still wanted her, period.

"You haven't run any of this by Natalie yet?" Tracker asked.

"No."

Tracker grinned. "I'd say you have your work cut out for you—on more than one front. She struck me as the straight-as-an-arrow type and I don't have to tell you that you've always taken the riskier approach."

"Yeah." Tracker was the one who'd nicknamed him "Chance" when they'd worked together in a Special Forces unit.

"Have you got a plan?"

"Not yet." Three days ago, he'd called her department, but at the last minute, he'd asked to talk to her partner, Matt Ramsey, instead.

"She didn't strike me as the type who could be easily conned," Tracker said, his grin widening.

"No." Chance bit back a sigh. If he was going to convince Natalie Gibbs to join him, he was going to have to pull off some fancy moves all right. And so far, he hadn't come up with a plan that had a chance in hell of succeeding.

"Tell you what," Tracker said. "Sophie's throwing a party at her antique shop on Friday to showcase some local artists. Natalie will be there. Why don't you come?"

Chance thought for a minute. If he ran into Natalie at a party, she couldn't refuse to see him. She'd have no choice but to talk to him at least.

"I'll take you up on that," Chance said. That gave him about forty-eight hours to come up with a strategy. Deadlines always sparked his creativity.

"Good. I was sure I was going to be bored. Now, I'll have the chance to observe a master con man at work."

"Here are the latest acceptances to your party."

Carlo Brancotti didn't glance up from his computer screen as his personal assistant, Lisa McGill, placed a manila folder on his desk. He was a careful man. Some judged him to be too careful, but he hadn't remained at the top of his profession by letting down his guard. Anything out of the ordinary was reported to him instantly, and his surveillance team had phoned him the minute the boat had been spotted so close to shore. They'd already traced the license plate. It belonged to Lucas Wainwright. Frowning, he tapped his fingers on his desk. Wainwright…the name was familiar, but the details escaped him.

Suddenly, the information appeared on the screen. Carlo scanned it quickly. Lucas Wainwright, CEO of Wainwright Enterprises, owner of a resort hotel in the Keys and another in South Beach, frequently used his boat to fish.

Satisfied, Carlo turned his attention to Lisa. "Report."

"All of the usuals, Sir Arthur and Lady Latham, the Moto brothers, the Demirs and Hassam Aldiri."

"And the first-timers?"

Lisa frowned a bit. First-timers made her nervous because there was a chance, always a chance, that one of them would be a plant, someone that a big insurance company or a law enforcement agency had gotten to. Carlo was looking forward to that very possibility. Foiling those who thought they could catch him was half the fun of the business he was in. More than anything, he enjoyed the game. He always had. The money was just a very pleasant side benefit.

"Risa Manwaring, Armand Genovese and Steven Bradford have all accepted, and they will arrive on Sunday."

The disapproval in her voice had him biting back a smile as he opened the file she'd placed on his desk. He wouldn't show any disapproval for her concern, for it was her job to worry and to keep him safe. "You've put them under surveillance?"

"Of course."

Carlo nodded in approval as he examined the photos in the file. Lisa had already run background checks on all three—Risa Manwaring, the retired film star, who now lived in seclusion; Armand Genovese, the Italian businessman, with rumored ties to organized crime; and Steven Bradford, the software genius, who reportedly had money to burn. Each would have his or her own reasons for wanting to acquire the Ferrante diamond. Which one, he wondered, would have that special craving for it that would run up the price?

Taking out the photos, he lined them up in a neat row, then pulled a magnifying glass from his desk. Not one of them offered a clear, accurate image. "These were the best you could get hold of?"

"Yes. I'm still working on it."

He nodded in approval, but he didn't expect her to find any better pictures of his future guests. He'd chosen these three specifically because all three shunned the media.

Which one would the man who called himself Chance Mitchell be impersonating? That was the question.

There wasn't a doubt in his mind that the insurance agent who'd come so close to tripping him up on his last job would take the bait. The man was good. Too good. After their last encounter, Carlo had made it his business to learn everything he could about the freelance insurance investigator who went by the name of Chance.

Carlo doubted that was the man's real name or that he even used it very often. There was even a possibility that Chance was a woman. In the past seven years, Chance Mitchell had become a legend of sorts in certain circles, the one person feared by anyone in Carlo's business.

But Carlo wasn't afraid. No, indeed, he thought as he smiled. He was looking forward to going up against Chance Mitchell again. Lately, he'd found that life offered too few challenges. With one long finger, he tapped each of the photos in turn. Which one would Chance choose to appear as? Risa, Armand, Steven or the woman on Steven's arm? He lowered the magnifying glass to decipher the name. Calli.

"Run a check on this Calli also."

"Yes, sir," Lisa replied.

Carlo set down the magnifying glass. He would know each one of his invited guests intimately before they arrived at his estate. Which one would turn out to be the one he would have to kill?

3

NATALIE SPOTTED her sisters the moment she stepped into the Blue Pepper. Rory, as usual, was in the thick of things, having an animated conversation with the reservation hostess. Natalie had no doubt that in spite of the crowd, Rory would get them a table. With her pixie face and short, dark hair, Rory had always reminded Natalie of Puck, the mischievous fairy in Shakespeare's *A Midsummer Night's Dream*. She had a knack for muddling things up the same way he had.

As Natalie edged her way through the crowd, she searched for a glimpse of her youngest sister, Sierra. Sure enough, Sierra was seated next to the reservation desk, looking on and jotting something down on one of the blue note cards she never seemed to be without. Natalie bit back a sigh.

With her straight blond hair and innocent air, Sierra had always made Natalie think of Alice in Wonderland. Though the academic Sierra was more intellectual than Alice and more shy, she was every bit as curious. However, Sierra never ever just tumbled into things the way Alice had. Instead, from the time she was little, she'd mapped out everything she did on blue note cards.

Well, Natalie believed in plans, too, but she drew the line at listing steps on note cards of any color. And she worried a bit that Sierra, who'd been sick a lot as a child, was a little too organized and too cautious in her approach to life. But whenever she broached the subject to Sierra, her sister would point out that her planning had gotten her two Ph.D. degrees and a tenure-track position at Georgetown University.

Ever since their father had left them, Natalie had always believed that it was her job to look out for her sisters, and she couldn't help worrying about how they were going to take the news that she was bringing them tonight.

Outside on the patio, a saxophonist blew a trill of notes, and Natalie stopped short as the image of Chance Mitchell slipped, unwanted, into her mind. That was all it took for her body to respond. Annoyance streamed through her. It had been three months since she'd been here with him—three long months since she'd thrown caution to the winds and spent the night with him. And she still couldn't get him out of her mind.

One night. That's what he'd offered and what she'd agreed to. He'd promised no-strings, no-etiquette sex, and he'd certainly delivered. Just the memory of what he'd done to her, what they'd done to each other, was enough to have her skin heating and something deep inside of her melting.

It certainly wasn't Chance's fault that she'd never before experienced anything like it. Nor could she in all fairness blame him for the fact that she wanted to experience it again.

Her glance shifted to the patio where they'd danced and where he'd made her the proposition. Oh, there was a part of her that wanted to blame Chance, a part of her that wanted to pay him back for the fact that since she'd spent that one freeing night with him, she'd felt restless, unsatisfied with her job and with her life.

And dammit, she'd been perfectly satisfied before. Her work on a select task force that handled high profile crimes in D.C. was exciting, but lately she was… just plain bored.

"Detective Natalie! Greetings, greetings, greetings."

Natalie smiled at Rad as he rushed up, grabbed her hands and rained kisses on the air several inches above her knuckles. The young restaurant owner was a full head shorter than she was, and he changed his hair color as frequently as he changed his ties. Tonight he was wearing his pale blond hair in spikes that were tipped with orange. She noted that the shade matched one of the swirls in his psychedelic tie.

Holding her hands a few inches out from her sides, Rad's smile faded as he gave her outfit a thorough look. The linen suit she wore was khaki colored, the T-shirt beneath was black, and she could sense a fashion critique coming her way.

"How's George?" she asked in an effort to deflect Rad's attention. George, Rad's partner, was a bronze-skinned, gentle giant of a man who managed the bar while Rad ran the restaurant.

Rad waved a hand. "George is gorgeous. Perfect, as usual. You, on the other hand…" He broke off to press a hand over his heart. "It cuts me to the quick to see you in such drab colors. Aquamarine would do wonders for you. Or mint-green." He tapped a finger to his lips as he considered. "No, pink. You should really think *pink*."

Natalie suppressed a shudder. A cop wearing pink? Not to mention what the color would look like in contrast to her red hair. She thought not. In a second attempt to distract Rad, she said, "Nice hairdo."

He flashed her a grin. "Thanks. There's a lot of product up there."

"Excellent match with the tie."

Rad fluttered his hand an inch above the spikes. "I had to work on the color for over an hour. I could do something quite wonderful with yours."

"I'd rather you found me a table."

Rad glanced over to where Rory was beaming at the reservation hostess. "I think your sister has taken care of that. I'll run interference for you."

Straightening her shoulders, Natalie followed Rad through the crowd. Tonight she and her sisters were going to celebrate their mutual birthdays, and she was bringing them a surprise present.

The envelope she carried in her purse had arrived this morning. It had contained a note from her father's attorney and three separate sealed envelopes for Harry Gibbs's daughters. Inside were messages from their father—messages that he'd written six years ago and had wanted them to read on their twenty-sixth birthday.

All day long the letters had been weighing on her mind and her heart. She still wasn't sure how she felt about them. Harry Gibbs had walked out on his family when she and her sisters were ten years old. When they were twenty, he'd died in a fluke climbing accident. Her father had always been taking risks. Within six months of receiving the news of Harry Gibbs's death, their mother had died, too.

Natalie had always known that her parents had loved one another—and there wasn't a doubt in her mind that her mother had died of a broken heart. But ten years before their deaths, Harry and Amanda Gibbs had split up because of "irreconcilable differences."

In this case the difference they couldn't reconcile was the fact that Harry Gibbs was a master jewel thief who found it impossible to settle down, and their mother Amanda wanted to raise her daughters in a stable, conservative environment.

Six years ago their father had suddenly decided to send them some kind of message they would receive on their twenty-sixth birthday? Personally, Natalie felt half pissed and half saddened by that, and she suspected that her sisters would feel the same.

Just then, Rory spotted her and called out, "Nat! This way."

Not content with waiting for Natalie to reach them, Rory grabbed Sierra by the hand and began to muscle her way through the crowd. The picture that they made moving toward her was one she'd seen so often—Rory rushing forward and Sierra having to be dragged along. Natalie had sometimes wondered why Rory hadn't made it first out of the womb.

"Happy birthday," Natalie said when they reached her.

"Happy birthday," Rory echoed.

"Ditto," Sierra said as they exchanged hugs.

"It's not every day we all turn twenty-six," Rory said in an undertone. "When I explained it to the hostess, she agreed that we should have a table on the patio. C'mon."

The patio was the last place Natalie wanted to be, but she didn't have the heart to spoil Rory's delight with herself. Still, as they moved down the short flight of stairs, she had to put some effort into keeping her eyes from straying to the spot behind the potted trees where Chance had drawn her to make his proposition.

"You all right?" Sierra asked as they followed Rory across the dance floor.

Natalie managed a smile. "Absolutely. How's the research going, Dr. Gibbs?"

"It's going. Of course, all the data isn't in yet."

"Don't pay any attention to her. Her research is going brilliantly," Rory said. "It always does. The big news is that my job at *Celebs* magazine is going well. A first for me. There's a senior reporter there who's taken me under her wing and I'm really enjoying the work."

"This calls for champagne," Sierra said.

"Agreed," Rory said as she sat down and picked up a menu. "And I'm starved."

Natalie waited until they were all seated before she said, "Maybe we ought to hold off on the celebration."

"What is it?" Sierra asked.

As Natalie explained the package she'd received that morning, she took the sealed envelopes out of her purse and placed them on the table. For a moment, all three of them simply stared at the white rectangles.

"To open them or not to open them, that is the question," Sierra finally said.

"Exactly." Natalie could always depend on that fine analytical mind of Sierra's to cut to the bottom line.

"They're from our father," Rory pointed out.

"So what?" Natalie said, letting a little of her anger show. "We agreed to stop calling him 'father' when we were ten because he left us."

Silence stretched between them again.

"It's been sixteen years since we last saw him and six years since he died." Sierra placed one finger on the corner of her envelope. "Why now?"

"Exactly," Natalie said again. "He's never once gotten in touch with us—not when we were sick, not for a birthday or a graduation. Not for anything. Why did he instruct the attorney to get those letters to us now?"

A waiter appeared, pen poised at the ready. "Drink orders, ladies?"

"A martini," Natalie said without taking her eyes off the envelopes. "Very dry with an olive."

"I'll have what she's having," Sierra said.

Rory sighed. "Ditto. Champagne just isn't going to do it. And bring us one of those appetizer samplers with three of everything. I'm definitely going to need food before I deal with this."

After the waiter hurried off, the silence descended again for a moment.

"Neither of you has to deal with this right now," Natalie finally said. "But I think I do have to open mine. I've got too much of Harry in me just to throw it away."

"We all have too much of Harry in us," Rory said.

Sierra drew in a quick hitched breath and let it out. "I'm afraid to open mine."

Natalie reached for her sister's hand. "Are you all right? Do you need your inhaler?"

Sierra shook her head. "I'm not having an asthma attack. I'm just a coward."

"No, you're not." Natalie and Rory spoke in unison.

"Tell you what," Natalie said. "We'll make a plan and you can jot it down on one of those note cards."

Rory nodded in agreement. "Even I could use some kind of plan for this."

Sierra pulled a blue card out of the canvas bag she always carried with her.

"We'll go in the order of our births. I'll go first," Natalie said.

Rory patted Sierra's arm. "Number one—Natalie, our fearless leader. And put me down for the number two slot."

"And I'm number three," Sierra said as she added her name to the list.

"And I'm the only one who's going to open her letter tonight." Though Natalie could sense that Rory might want to open hers tonight, she willed her to go along. "The two of you can wait. For a few weeks, a year, five years—take all the time you need. Harry certainly took his time getting these to us."

"Good plan," Rory said.

As Natalie slipped a finger under the flap, she could see some of the tension fade in the way Sierra was gripping her pencil. Finessing the envelope open, she took out the letter. Then clearing her throat, she read it out loud.

Dearest Natalie, my warrior and seeker of justice, Happy birthday. You're probably wondering why I'm sending you this letter on this particular birthday, and the answer is a bit complicated. Your mother and I were exactly twenty-six when you came into our lives. Ten years later, I gave you up. Your mother and I agreed when we separated that I would cut off any contact with you until you were twenty-six. We thought that was for the best. I now know that leaving you and leaving your mother was the biggest mistake I ever made. If something happens to me and I can't be with you on your twenty-sixth birthday, I want you to know this: Don't make the same mistake that I did. When you see what you want, trust in your talents. Risk anything it takes to get it. And most importantly, hold on to it.

Love,
Harry

"Well," Rory said.

Natalie placed the letter down on the table and ran her finger over the signature. She couldn't put a name to any of the feelings swirling through her. "You've got to hand it to him—he's a man who walked his talk. He went for what he wanted, and we all paid the price."

"Look." Sierra pointed at the envelope. "There's something else inside."

Natalie pulled out three photos. One was taken at her high school graduation, another on her first day at the police academy. The third one was from when she was twelve, and she'd had to stay in the hospital over-night to have her tonsils out.

"He was there," Rory said. "I'd figured he'd forgotten all about us."

Sierra studied the photos when Natalie passed them to her. "I'd always suspected that he and Mom made some sort of deal that he had to stay away. She was so afraid that we would take after him."

"And now he seems to be advising you to do just that," Natalie said. "'Trust in your talents…risk anything it takes….'"

"That's exactly what you want to do, isn't it?" Sierra asked as the waiter set their drinks and a platter of appetizers in front of them. "That's what's been bothering you for the past three months, right?"

Natalie stared at her. Sierra was the most observant of her sisters, but Natalie hadn't thought she'd been that transparent. "I don't want to become a jewel thief, if that's what you're asking."

"But…" Sierra urged.

Natalie sighed and turned to Rory. "It was a mistake to let her get that Ph.D. in psychology."

"You're just evading the issue," Rory said around a mouthful of shrimp. "You haven't been yourself lately. Even I've noticed that. But I don't think it's because you're thinking of ditching law enforcement for a career in grand larceny. I'm betting it's a man."

"I've sworn off," Natalie said with a frown.

"Here, here." Rory lifted her glass. "I'll drink to that. Ever since Paul the jerk dumped me, I've decided that the only men I'll allow in my life are the ones I create in my fantasies."

Sierra laughed and joined in the toast. "Which particular man have you sworn off, Nat?"

Natalie slanted Sierra a look. "You should have been a cop." Then with a sigh, she set down her glass. Who better to talk to than her two sisters? "The man is the one I worked with on that smuggling case three months ago. I haven't been able to get him out of my mind."

"So what's the problem?" Rory asked. "I've never known you to have any trouble getting a man if you wanted him?"

Natalie turned to face her two sisters. "That's just it. I don't want to want him. Besides, the feeling doesn't seem to be mutual. I haven't heard from him in three months. Not that I expected to. We had an agreement—for one night. That was all."

"That is a problem," Sierra said.

Natalie sighed. "That's not the only one. Ever since I worked with him on that case, I've begun to be restless at my job. I've been grumpy with my partner, Matt, my office seems to be closing in on me and I want more than anything to escape."

Shocked at what she'd just admitted, Natalie stared at her two sisters and found them staring right back at her. "I am just like Harry."

"Of course, you're like him," Rory said, helping herself to a crab puff. "We try to deny it, but we're all like him. I count on luck to get me out of scrapes. Sierra uses that marvelous brain she inherited from him. And you take the risks that he thrived on, though you try very hard to keep a lid on that tendency. But, face it, we can't escape our genes."

"Sierra," Natalie said, "you want to help me out on this one? Tell her she's wrong."

Sierra shook her head. "I can't. Rory's right. We are, all of us, his daughters—for better or worse. But if you want my advice…"

"I need something," Natalie said, waving away the shrimp that Rory offered her. "And I don't mean food."

"I think that you ought to follow his advice. You've seen what you want. Why not trust in your talents and take a risk?" Sierra said.

Natalie turned her gaze to Rory.

"You're not going to get any argument from me. You like this guy who hasn't called you in three months. I say go get him. And if you want to give up your job as a cop, do that, too. For years, you've been the responsible one, holding down a steady job, helping Sierra apply to another graduate school, helping me write yet another résumé. But Sierra and I are officially all grown-up now. You can stop worrying about us and escape."

"I'm not giving up my job." The thought had a little curl of panic tightening in her stomach. "I heard this afternoon that he's going to be at the party Sophie Wainwright is throwing at her shop on Friday."

"Excellent," Rory said. "Sierra was invited, and she's bringing me as her guest. We'll be there to cheer you on."

Natalie drew in a deep breath, then let it out. "I'm just not sure.…"

"Do you want him?" Rory asked.

"Yes." She couldn't deny that. It had been three months, and she hadn't gotten him out of her head.

Rory selected another mushroom. "Then I say follow Harry's advice and take a risk. What have you got to lose?"

Natalie said nothing as the curl of panic tightened in her stomach. As a cop, she was used to facing her fears. As a woman, she was less sure of herself. Except for that night she'd spent with Chance. She lifted her hands and dropped them. "We had an agreement—for one night."

"Agreements can be renegotiated." Rory sipped her martini.

"Whose idea was it to make it one night?" Sierra asked.

"His," Natalie replied.

"Figures," Rory said.

"In many primitive cultures, the woman is the hunter when it comes to mate selection," Sierra said.

"Whoa." Natalie lifted her hands, palm outward. "I'm not on the hunt for a mate. I'm more in the mood for a fling. And I was in total agreement about the one night."

"And all you want is one more night?" Sierra asked.

"Yeah," Natalie said. One more night. Maybe then, she could get him out of her system and get her life back to normal.

Sierra cleared her throat. "Then I have a suggestion. For my current research project, I've been researching the sexual fantasies of different cultures."

"That's our girl," Rory said, lifting her glass.

After they toasted again, Sierra continued, "One of

the most universal fantasies is sex with a stranger—
someone you don't know and never will know." Pausing, she cleared her throat again. "So why don't you
just pretend that you're someone else for the night?"

When her two sisters turned to stare at her, Sierra
hurried on. "It makes sense. You love undercover work
and you're good at it. So just come to Sophie's party
as someone else."

"That's a great idea," Rory said, waving a shrimp.

"I don't think—"

"That's your problem, Nat," Rory said. "You over-
think everything. Sierra's got a great idea."

"You're so good at disguise," Sierra continued.
"You could just let yourself *be* this other person. That
way you can put Natalie Gibbs's fears and hang-ups
away for the evening and be free to make a play for
this man as a totally different person."

"You're serious, aren't you?" Natalie asked.

"Absolutely." Sierra leaned forward. "It's the age-
old concept of Mardi Gras. For one night you put on
a mask and do things that you would never do as your
real self. Very freeing."

Rory shot Natalie a look. "Freeing? Does this sound
like the baby sister we used to know and love?"

Natalie shook her head, seriously considering her
youngest sister's idea. She glanced down at her drink.
The glass was still half-full, so she couldn't blame the
martini. Her gaze shifted to the letter and her father's
words.

*When you see what you want, trust in your talents.
Risk anything it takes...*

Natalie ran her finger over her father's signature

again. She wanted Chance, and if she took Sierra's suggestion, she could go after him with a clean slate. She wouldn't be Natalie, the woman he hadn't called for three months.

"Think about it," Sierra said.

If she did decide to follow Sierra's advice, she knew two things for sure. Chance Mitchell wouldn't recognize her. And he wouldn't know what hit him.

CHANCE STOOD outside on the flagstone patio at the back of Sophie Wainwright's antique and collectibles shop and scanned the crowd through the window. From what he could see, the event was a success. Three musicians were tucked away in a corner playing Mozart, and a white-jacketed waiter offering flutes of champagne was threading his way through the crush of guests.

In between the potted trees and terra-cotta urns bursting with pansies and geraniums, Chance spotted a prominent senator, a congresswoman and several well-heeled collectors who'd been frequent clients at the gallery down the street where he'd worked undercover.

The person he hadn't spotted yet was Natalie Gibbs. He'd told himself that he came through the back alleyway because of the line of guests waiting to get in the front door of the shop, but the truth was he was stalling. He still wasn't sure how he was going to handle Natalie when he ran into her.

Damn if his hands weren't damp. With a frown, he rubbed them on his pants. A woman hadn't made him nervous since junior high school. He'd spent two days thinking of ways to convince her to go with him on the Florida caper. The best scenario he'd come up with was to play it by ear. Not that he was worried about that part. He wasn't a planner by nature, and he'd gotten himself out of plenty of scrapes by improvising. He wasn't worried about the job—she'd come with him to Florida, all right. It was on the personal level that he wasn't quite sure how to handle Natalie Gibbs.

Later, he couldn't have said what it was that drew his gaze to the small balcony on the second story of Sophie's shop. But the moment he saw the woman, he felt his mind go blank and then fill with her. Her hair was blond, parted in the middle, and it fell in a straight, smooth curve almost to her shoulders. The tiny black dress revealed curves in all the right places and left more bare than it covered. The summer sky was finally beginning to darken overhead, but even in the less than perfect light her skin had the pale perfection of an old-fashioned cameo. Chance let out a breath he hadn't known he was holding.

She was the kind of woman who would get a second glance from any man, but Chance couldn't seem to get past the first one. The quick tightening in his gut was unexpectedly raw and hot, but what surprised him most was the flicker of familiarity, recognition almost, that pushed at the edges of his mind. He could have sworn he'd never laid eyes on her before. If he had, he certainly would have remembered.

And then her eyes met his, and for the second time in as many moments, Chance felt his mind empty. The primitive streak of desire that moved through him had him scanning the iron railing, looking for a staircase,

a ladder—or tree branch that extended far enough to…
He hadn't realized that he'd moved closer to the balcony until he bumped smack into a waiter. The man's tray tilted, two champagne flutes began a downward slide. Chance barely managed to catch them.

"Sorry," he murmured as he settled them on the tray.

"No problem, sir."

"I'll take one of those, if you don't mind." He took a long swallow of the icy wine before he raised his gaze to the balcony again.

She was gone.

Disappointment warred with astonishment. Had he really been thinking of doing the Romeo thing and scaling a balcony? What in hell was the matter with him? Shakespeare's star-crossed hero had been all of about sixteen. Chance was twice that age. Hormone-driven foolishness was a thing of his adolescent past. Or it should be.

Still there was some similarity between Romeo and himself, he thought as his lips curved in amusement. In a way, he *was* crashing a party. He hadn't gotten an engraved invitation from Sophie, merely a verbal, secondhand one from his friend Tracker. But that's where the parallel would end. He hadn't come here to meet some woman he was going to lust after at first sight and then fall madly and tragically in love with.

He was here to make an offer to Natalie Gibbs that she would not be able to refuse. Taking another sip from his glass, Chance made his way to the French doors that opened into the shop. But it took more effort than he liked not to glance back up at the balcony.

4

WITH A HAND firmly pressed against the nerves jittering in her stomach, Natalie closed the door to the balcony behind her and took two steps into the office above Sophie's shop.

So much for the hope that the attraction she felt for Chance Mitchell had faded with time and distance. His absence from her life might not have made her heart grow fonder, but it had sure increased the lust factor.

One look, one meeting of eyes at a distance of some twenty feet had her nipples tightening and muscles she hadn't even known she had clenching deep inside of her. If he could do that to her with a look, what would happen if he touched her, kissed her, made love to her again? At the image that filled her mind, an arrow of pleasure, hot and sweet, streaked right to her center. Natalie lowered her hand from her stomach to the spot where she throbbed and reminded herself to breathe.

There was no need to panic. She could handle this—because she was Rachel Cade. Drawing in a deep breath, she moved toward the antique mirror in the far corner of the room. All she had to do was get into character the way she did for a job. She met the eyes of the woman who stared back at her from the silvered glass and let the tension ease from her shoulders. She could barely recognize Natalie Gibbs at all. Rachel Cade had straight blond hair. Natalie's hair was red and had a tendency to curl. Rachel's eyes were blue. Natalie's were green. Rachel was wearing a dress—what there was of it—that Natalie never would have bought.

In front, the thin black silk covered her from breast to midthigh, and the back was bare from neck to waist except for a narrow strap that went over the shoulder. Oh my, no. She smiled at her reflection. Natalie Gibbs would never have worn this dress because she held men at arm's length and dressing like this would have been counterproductive.

Rachel Cade didn't have any hang-ups about men. Thank heavens! With a smile, she watched Rachel push her hair back behind her ears. It wasn't a wig. Midsummer in D.C. was far too hot for that. So she'd had it dyed and flat-ironed. Her hairdresser had had to double up on his anxiety medication, but she'd been firm about the color change. Besides, if she was going to take Sierra's advice and *be* someone else, even for a short period of time, she was going to go all the way. For the next few days, she *was* Rachel Cade. She'd arranged to take the time off that her partner, Matt Ramsey, had been pushing her to enjoy. No sense in doing something unless you were willing to *risk anything it takes*.

She shook her head and watched her hair settle back into place. This was her chance to see if blondes really did have more fun and if gentlemen preferred them.

After fishing lip gloss out of her bag, she slicked

it on. This was what she'd always most enjoyed about being a cop—the opportunity it gave her to become someone else for a while. It was a weakness, she knew, but it was also very liberating. And becoming Rachel Cade was especially so. When she did under-cover work, the persona she created was often dic-tated by the job, but she'd had complete freedom with Rachel. The tall blonde staring back at her from the mirror was a distant cousin of the Gibbs sisters. She'd come from her home in South Florida to visit for two weeks.

Natalie had never been to South Florida in her life, so she'd read up on it. Not that she expected Chance to give her a pop quiz, but in a good undercover oper-ation, one always had to be prepared, just in case.

Just thinking about him had an image of Chance slipping into her mind. The tuxedo he was wearing cer-tainly enhanced that long rangy body….

No. She wasn't going to go there, or she'd be stuck in this room all night imagining what it would be like to get her hands on him again. Natalie might be satis-fied with a fantasy life, but Rachel preferred the real thing. She gave herself one last glance in the mirror as she reviewed her plan. Rachel Cade—blond ambition and material girl all rolled into one—wanted to have a hot, wild and mutually satisfying night—or two or three—with Chance Mitchell. He would have fun. She would have fun. And they could go their separate ways.

Luckily, that would never bother a girl like Rachel. She would just move on to the next man. Oh, she was going to like being Rachel Cade. After beaming one last smile at the girl in the mirror, Natalie walked to the door.

"YOU DON'T LOOK like you're having a very good time."

As usual, Chance hadn't seen or heard his friend Tracker approach. "I haven't yet spotted my quarry."

"She'll be here. Her sisters arrived about twenty minutes ago with a cousin who's visiting from South Florida. Sophie took them on a quick tour. She's outdone herself with this place, don't you think?"

Chance glanced at his friend, intrigued by his tone that contained a mix of pride, approval, and… Searching for a word, all he could come up with was loyalty. "You haven't even tied the knot yet, and you're beginning to sound like an old married man."

"Yeah." A man of few words, Tracker thought for a minute. "Yeah." He didn't sound a bit displeased. "By the way, I developed those pictures we took on our fishing trip. Looks like there are only the two sentry stations we spotted, but I'm betting he has other guards patrolling the beach. It won't be a piece of cake, but I can get you off the place by water. Any word on when you leave?"

"Day after tomorrow."

Tracker shot him a look. "You're cutting it close. What if Natalie doesn't agree to go?"

"I'll just have to make her an offer she can't refuse." Chance's gaze drifted to the flight of stairs that ran up the far wall of the store. He knew there was one display room on the second floor and another, smaller space where Sophie kept an office. His mystery woman had to be up there.

"Natalie's sisters are right over there if you want to ask them when she's expected to arrive."

Dragging his eyes from the stairs, Chance shifted his attention to where Tracker was pointing.

"The blonde is the academic," Tracker said. "Her name's Sierra and Mac says that there was quite a buzz when both the anthropology department and the psychology department at Georgetown hired her. And the short dark-haired one is Rory. She's a freelance writer. If you want, I can introduce you— Uh-oh, Sophie's giving me a signal. You're on your own."

The moment Tracker began to make his way through the crowd, Chance opted to edge his way along the wall to where the two Gibbs sisters were standing and surveying the party. But reaching them was easier said than done. Two major hurdles stood in his path—a group of women and a tall potted tree. He began to edge his way around the women.

"This is such a crush," a tall brunette said. "I'm going to have to come back when I can really see this place."

"Me, too," another woman said.

"Look, over there. Isn't that Mame Appelgate who writes a column for the *Washington Post?* All it will take is a mention from her, and it'll be a crush here tomorrow, too."

Chance found himself temporarily wedged between the wall and a potted palm. Through the leaves, he could see Sierra's cheeks were flushed, and she shook her head as Rory offered her something from the well-stocked plate she was holding.

"I can't eat," Sierra said.

"Relax. Natalie will be fine," Rory managed around a mouthful of pastry.

Sierra glanced at her watch. "I think you should go upstairs and check on her."

Though he hadn't meant to eavesdrop, Chance moved closer.

"Uh-uh. I value my life too much," Rory said. "Besides, she said she only needed a few minutes to get in character. You know Nat. She doesn't like to appear as a new 'persona' until the disguise is perfect and she's had a chance to assume her new persona. Harry was like that, too. Remember the game he played with us when he would show up at the door and we wouldn't be able to figure out who he was?"

"Nat always knew," Sierra said.

"Just like I always knew when he was bluffing at poker." Rory paused with a shrimp halfway to her mouth to sigh. "You know, I still miss him."

"Me, too," Sierra said. "Have you thought about when you're going to open your letter?"

"No. I figure I'll know when the time is right. But I'm going to wait until Natalie has had her adventure. I'll need both of you there when I do."

"Yes," Sierra agreed. "I will, too."

Rory studied the food on her plate and then offered it to Sierra again. "Come on. You'll feel better if you eat something."

"I'm too nervous," Sierra said. "I just feel so responsible for this. I suggested the plan."

Rory reached out a hand to pat her sister's arm. "I'm sure Dr. Frankenstein felt the same way right after he threw the electrical switch for the first time."

"Not funny."

Rory rolled her eyes. "Nat is going to be fine. And your plan is brilliant. Pretending to be someone else is the perfect ticket for her. For a little while, she can leave all of her responsibilities behind and be someone entirely different. As soon as my job at *Celebs* is more secure, I may try a masquerade thing myself." She tossed a morsel of food into her mouth. You've really got to try these crab puffs."

Masquerade. Chance tried to make sense of the thoughts swirling through his mind as he replayed the snatch of conversation he'd just heard. Natalie Gibbs was adopting a new persona? She was going to be someone else for a while? Chance scanned the crowd, this time more carefully than he had before. He'd seen Natalie Gibbs in an undercover disguise twice. She was good, but he should be able to spot her.

He made one full circuit of the store and came up empty. Frustrated, he moved out onto the patio. Immediately, a ripple of awareness moved through him. Natalie. But when he turned, it wasn't Natalie he saw. It was his blond mystery woman from the balcony. Even then, he might have continued his search for Natalie. But the blonde chose that particular moment to shove her hair behind her ear, something that he'd seen Natalie Gibbs do countless times. He dropped his gaze to her feet. Sure enough, one of them was tapping. That was another habit Natalie had.

Then he simply stared. Could it be? Was this the disguise that Sierra and Rory had been referring to? Could his blond mystery woman be Natalie Gibbs?

Chance accepted a drink from a passing waiter and

sipped without tasting what he'd chosen. He had to think, and the first step would be to unglue his eyes from his mystery woman's legs. He was not going to find the answer to his question there. He shifted his gaze slowly upward.

Gestures aside, this woman was a sharp right turn from the Natalie Gibbs he knew. But his gut instinct, which rarely failed him, was telling him that the detective he was searching for and the blonde he was looking at were one and the same person. The light was no better than it had been before, but he was closer, and there was no balcony blocking his view.

Over the years, he'd honed his observation skills, but they'd seldom brought him more pleasure. Her eyes were heavy-lidded, her mouth slick and cherry-red. During the time he'd spent with Natalie, she'd either been disguised as a man, or had been wearing muted makeup colors. He wasn't close enough to make out the color of her eyes. Natalie's, he recalled, were a deep shade of bottomless green, but he was willing to bet that the blonde's were a different color. When a professional put on a new persona, he or she went all the way and changed everything that could possibly be changed.

Like the hair. Natalie's was red and long and curly. He'd thought of an exploding sunset the first time he'd seen it. The blonde's hair, shorter and straight, with the finish of newly spun silk, held its own attraction. The slick fall of it tempted a man to touch, and once he did, there would be all that smooth skin to explore. Then there were those legs—his gaze slipped back to them. They were nothing short of miraculous.

It occurred to him that he'd never seen what Natalie Gibbs looked like in a dress because she'd always hidden her feminine figure beneath trousers and a jacket. His mystery woman didn't seem to believe in hiding anything. The contrasts fascinated him. Natalie Gibbs was all work. His mystery woman shouted "play." Detective Gibbs's sex appeal, out of sight beneath pantsuits, was muted like the steady hum of a current along a wire. The blonde's sex appeal snapped and crackled around her like static electricity.

A man was bound to be burned if he got too close. And he was being drawn as inevitably as a moth. He'd already moved halfway across the patio toward her, and he still hadn't decided how he was going to handle her. Oh, this was Natalie Gibbs all right. Hadn't he known it on some level from the first moment he'd spotted her and felt that tiny click of recognition? This Natalie was the one he'd discovered when they'd made love in her apartment that night three months ago.

Just what kind of a game was she playing?

A warning voice told him to wait until he'd weighed his options and come up with a strategy. But the inner voice he'd always trusted was reminding him that he did his best work when he played it by ear.

5

NATALIE KNEW the moment that Chance spotted her, and she struggled to keep the tension out of her shoulders. It was bad enough that her stomach was jittering again.

She could feel his eyes on her and sensed the instant they moved from her face down her body to her legs. Though it took some effort, she stopped tapping her foot. He was sharp, and he knew all about disguises. This would be the supreme test of just how good her persona was. She signaled a passing waiter and took a glass of champagne. As yet no one had known who she really was.

As a preliminary test, she'd asked Sierra and Rory to introduce her to Tracker McBride and Sophie Wainwright. They'd been pleased to meet the Gibbs sisters' cousin, but she'd detected no gleam of recognition in their eyes.

When the short, bald man to her left said something, she shoved her hair behind her ear and smiled down at him. Before she could catch his name, she found herself surrounded by the two other men he was with. Instantly, she was ankle-deep—no, make that waist-deep—in a discussion of a new water pollution bill that was going to the house floor the next week. Because it was part of her job to know who was who in the nation's government, she recognized all three of the men. One was a congressman who'd been elected as an environmentalist; the two others were senators who had coauthored the bill under discussion.

"Darling, I've been looking all over for you," said a voice at her side. Then Chance took her arm in a firm grip, and shot a five-hundred-megawatt smile toward the three men who'd boxed her in. "Sorry, gentlemen, but I have to borrow back my wife. I have a proposition to make her. We're still newlyweds."

Natalie made no protest as Chance led her back into the store. Instead, she used the time to remind herself that she was Rachel. And Rachel Cade would never object to a man who looked like Chance leading her away. Nor would Rachel Cade care a fig if Chance Mitchell saw through her disguise. And any minute she would know if he had or not.

When he stopped in front of one of the display cases, he turned to her. "Aren't you even going to thank me?"

"For what?" she asked in the low voice she'd chosen for Rachel.

"I saved your life. Another five minutes and they would have bored you to death."

She felt her lips twitch, and some of her tension eased. She saw no hint of recognition in his expression. He hadn't seen through her *yet*. "What if I told you that I find environmental problems sexy?"

"I'd immediately find a job with the E.P.A."

She couldn't prevent the laugh, and she didn't stop

him when he placed a finger under her chin and tipped her face up so that their eyes met for the first time.

"Blue," he said. "I wondered."

For five whole seconds, Natalie held her breath. Chance's dark, smoky gray eyes held no knowing look. All she could see was curiosity...and the tiniest flare of heat. The heat she understood because his hand on her arm had created a flame that was spreading over her entire body. "Why did you wonder about my eyes?"

"Because I couldn't tell from across the room. Who are you?"

The blunt question had the rest of her nerves easing. He wasn't suspicious yet. It was up to her to make sure he stayed that way. "Rachel Cade."

He smiled and held out his hand. "Chance Mitchell."

She raised her brows. "Did I ask?"

Chance withdrew his extended hand and pulled an imaginary arrow out of his chest. "And after I saved your life."

Natalie laughed—not just because of what Chance had said but because she knew that she was in the clear. Her disguise was working, and she could feel the freedom move through her. If she were Natalie and Chance was flirting with her, she would make some excuse to leave and check on her sisters. But as Rachel she could eat it up. In fact, the only way to keep him believing in her persona was to do just that.

Chance reached over to tuck her hair behind her ear. "You know, I hate to use such a corny line, but when I first came in, I saw you standing on the balcony that overlooks the patio, and I thought for a moment that I'd seen you someplace before. Except if I had, I'm sure I would have remembered it."

The man had more than his share of charm. Natalie would have been wary of it. Rachel could simply enjoy it, just as she was enjoying the fact that his hand was still lingering on the sensitive skin behind her ear. "Nicely put. I'm told that I bear some resemblance to my cousins, the Gibbs triplets. Perhaps, that's what you see."

He studied her for a minute, and Natalie held her breath.

"Well, that's one mystery solved. On to another. Just who is Rachel Cade?"

Natalie smiled, trying not to let any trace show of the relief she was feeling. Now that the first hurdle had been cleared, it was time for step two of her plan. Seduce Chance Mitchell before he knew what hit him. She ran one finger down the lapel of his jacket.

"Who is Rachel Cade?" she repeated. Perhaps it was time to explore that question thoroughly. One thing she was discovering—Rachel wasn't nearly as patient as Natalie. And for some reason, Rachel seemed to be even more vulnerable to the attraction she was feeling for Chance. The moment he'd touched her, every nerve in her body had seemed to come alive. And the way he was looking at her now had her melting inside. She had a short bio all set to deliver, but suddenly she didn't want to waste the time. "That's a long, boring story. I can think of something we could do that would be much more fun than exchanging life stories."

CHANCE COULD almost hear some of the synapses in his brain disconnect. There wasn't much chance of making a snappy comeback when that happened. He heard his heart skip one full beat and then begin to pound until the noises of the party—the chatter, the clink of glasses, the music—all of it faded to a hum. And all the while, he simply couldn't take his eyes off of her. As if the combination of cherry-red lips and startlingly blue eyes weren't lethal enough, she now had a slew of very improper images flooding his mind. Thoroughly fascinated by this side of Natalie, he could barely wait to see what she would do next.

She filled in the silence by taking the fingers that were still at her ear and raising then to her mouth. He felt the warmth of her breath, then the cool brush of her lips just before the heat scorched through him. Even after she released his hand, he felt as if the skin had been singed by a candle.

"Where are you staying?" she asked.

"The Meridian," he said.

She ran one finger from his tie down the front of his shirt, stopping at the waistband of his pants. Then she traced the buckle of his belt. "You know, the moment I saw you, I thought to myself—when was the last time I made love with someone just for the fun of it? And I couldn't remember."

She was seducing him in the middle of a crowded party. And he wasn't doing a thing to stop her. He wasn't even taking over the task. He didn't want to. In some dark corner of his brain, Chance recalled that he'd come to this party with a job to do and that he was on a deadline. But none of that seemed to matter anymore.

Her fingers had slipped below his belt and were resting lightly on his erection. "Am I moving too fast for you? I have a tendency to do that."

"I think I can keep up."

She smiled at him. "Good. I'm only in town for a few days, and I'd hate to waste my time here."

"Time management just happens to be my specialty." Chance took the hand that was toying again with his belt and linked her fingers with his. "Let's go."

By the time he'd led her through the gate and down the alley to where he'd parked his car, he'd organized his thoughts a little. At least he thought he had. But when they reached the sleek red convertible, Natalie turned so her body brushed against his, and his brain seemed to switch off.

"You know, we're about to go off and have a bout of hot, wild sex," she said. "At least I hope we are. But we haven't even kissed yet. Maybe we ought to try it to see if we have the right chemistry."

Oh, they had the right chemistry all right. The luscious red lips were only inches away, and he was sure he could smell his synapses frying again. He had to get some kind of handle on his response to her.

He had not come to Sophie Wainwright's party to seduce Natalie Gibbs. He'd come to convince her to come to Florida with him. He needed her help, and what he was about to do might blow his chances of ever convincing her to help him catch Carlo Brancotti.

But from the moment she'd looked at him through those baby-blue contact lenses and told him that she wanted to do something a lot more fun than exchange life stories, he'd been unable to think about anything else. He might be about to make the biggest mistake of his life, but he wanted this Natalie just as desperately as he'd wanted the woman who'd haunted his dreams for the past three months.

But that didn't mean "Rachel" was going to have it all her way. Two could play the little game she'd started. He moved forward, just enough to push her back against the car and bring his body into full contact with hers. The quick hitch of her breath gave him a great deal of satisfaction. "If I kiss you now, really kiss you, I won't stop," he murmured, bringing his lips to within a breath of hers, "until I'm inside of you."

He saw the quick flash of heat in her eyes, felt it in the way her body melted against his. He rested his mouth against hers, just long enough to sample the yielding softness. Then he drew away. His words had conjured up in his mind a very clear image of what it would be like to take her right there on the hood of his car. He was ready. He'd been ready since he'd first spotted her on the balcony. And he could very easily find out if she was ready. All he had to do was slip his hand beneath the hem of her dress and up the satiny softness of her thigh. He had no doubt that she would be hot and wet and welcoming. The alley was deserted right now, and the party was in full swing. The sounds of string music and muted laughter carried clearly on the still night air.

When she looped her arms around his neck, and pulled his head just that little bit closer so that his lips were brushing hers again, he nearly gave in to the temptation to taste her. Later he would thank the blast of music from a car driving past the alley for saving them both. Placing his hands on her shoulders, he drew back. "We could get arrested."

"Arrested?" The cloudy mix of desire and confusion in her eyes nearly snapped his control.

"Yeah. Mug shots, fingerprints, one phone call. It could really take all the fun out of the evening."

"Yeah." She gave her head one quick shake to clear it, then pushed her hair behind her ear. Though he couldn't have said why, he found the nervous gesture endearing.

"I'll take a raincheck on that kiss," he said.

"Ditto."

He managed to get her into the car without touching her again. That was the easy part. The hard part was the drive to his hotel. They'd no sooner pulled out of the parking lot when she scrambled onto her knees and began to loosen his tie.

"Rachel, getting into an accident is another way to take the fun out of an evening."

Her laugh was quick and breathless in his ear. "I'm just trying to save us time. You did say you were into time management."

"Yeah." His tie was off, and her fingers were already slipping beneath the buttons of his shirt, leaving a trail of ice and heat on his skin. "Two rules. You keep your hands above my belt, and I'll promise to keep both of mine on the wheel."

Laughing, she closed her teeth around the lobe of his ear. "Deal. But don't they say rules are meant to be broken?"

NATALIE HADN'T convinced him to break the rules, but it had been a close call. She could tell by the quick way he handed the car keys over to a valet and drew her with him into the hotel. The Meridian was one of D.C.'s more posh accommodations for travellers. Many of the rooms boasted a view of the Washington Monument and the Mall, though she didn't think that she and Chance were going to spend time looking at either. She could feel heat radiating through her body from where his hand was pressed at the small of her back.

His touches, his kiss, had been tame so far, and she was beginning to crave him. When his body had brushed against hers in the parking lot, it had been hard, solid. In the three months since she'd last seen Chance, she'd spent some time imagining exactly what that body would feel like pressing into hers. Natalie, of course, had pushed those fantasies out of her mind. Rachel, on the other hand, couldn't wait to make those fantasies and more come true. Had Rachel always been living inside of her? That was something she would consider later. Right now, she was going to focus all her attention on Chance.

She said nothing until they were in the elevator and the doors were sliding shut. Then she turned to him. "Are you ever really going to kiss me?"

"Soon." He settled his hands at her waist, but instead of pulling her close, he turned her instead, so that she could see them both reflected in the mirrored walls of the elevator. Then meeting her eyes in the mirror, he moved one hand to her breast, the other to the hem of her dress. The sight of those long, lean fingers moving on her skin only doubled the sharp stab of pleasure moving through her. She was on fire where he touched her, and she was sure that her knees had turned to jelly.

"I've wanted to touch you like this ever since I first saw you on that balcony."

His fingers slipped beneath the bodice of the dress as his other hand began to push up the hem of her skirt. He moved so slowly. She wanted him to hurry. She wanted the sensations to go on forever. When her dress was up to her hips, he ran his finger along the lacy edge of her panties, from the top of her thigh to the narrow vee that disappeared between her legs. "When we were standing in the parking lot, I was tempted to do this."

Natalie watched his finger slip beneath the band of her panties.

"And this."

He pinched her nipple at the same time that he slipped a finger inside of her.

The orgasm that moved through her in one long, crashing wave had her sagging against him. Later, she couldn't recall exactly how they'd gotten out of the elevator and down the hall to the room. But by the time Chance had opened the door, she'd gotten some of her strength back. And she was thinking more clearly.

A sudden feeling of déjà vu struck her as he drew her into the narrow foyer. It grew sharper when he used his body to trap her against the wall. She recalled that he'd used the same move when they'd entered the tiny foyer of her apartment three months ago. He'd kissed her and then taken her, or they'd taken each other, on the floor.

Natalie had surrendered without a second thought,

just as she'd surrendered in the elevator a few seconds ago.

"Now, I'll kiss you," Chance said as he pressed his body more fully against hers.

But she didn't have to be Natalie. Tonight, she could be Rachel. Despite that her body was heating, melting against his, she avoided his mouth at the last moment. Her voice was breathless when she said, "Not yet. Turnabout's fair play. Now it's my turn to touch you."

6

BEMUSED, CHANCE STEPPED back and then followed Natalie into the sitting room of the suite.

"Ahhh. Mirrors. Just what I need." There was a wicked gleam in her eyes when she turned to face him.

Chance studied her for a moment. The woman in the elevator had been the Natalie who'd haunted his dreams for three months. He would have bet his life on it. But the woman who'd driven him crazy in the car and the woman facing him now was "Rachel." And he wanted her just as much.

He moved toward her, cupped a hand at the back of her neck. "I want you now."

She placed a hand on his chest with just enough pressure to preserve the distance between them. "You can have me. But what's the rush?"

His eyebrows rose. "You were in a hurry in the car."

She smiled up at him. "What happened in the elevator sort of took the edge off for me."

He increased the pressure on the back of her neck, and she moved closer so that her body was in contact with his.

"It only built the pressure for me."

"Yes, I can feel that. But I do have a solution."

He felt his heart quicken against her palm, saw her eyes darken when she felt its rapid beat, too. She slipped a finger beneath the top button of his shirt and freed it. "You're going to enjoy what I'm going to do to you. I promise."

Chance felt his mind begin to cloud as she continued to unbutton his shirt. Each time her fingers brushed against his skin, ribbons of heat fanned out across his skin. She pushed the shirt off of his shoulders and it slid to the floor.

"I wanted to do this right in front of everyone at Sophie Wainwright's party."

And she very nearly had, Chance recalled. Her hands were spread out along his waist now, and with her thumbs touching, she drew them upward over his ribs until they were resting just at the bottom of his rib cage.

"Watch what I'm doing in the mirror."

He could do that. His arms were beginning to feel heavy, but he could still move his eyes.

She rubbed her palms over his nipples and he sucked in a breath.

"You like that," she murmured as she did it again.

He felt his nipples harden. Her skin was so fair against the darker color of his. And the sensation—

"Let's try this." Leaning forward, she moistened one nipple and then the other with tongue. "I love your taste," she murmured then repeated the process.

His breath was backed up in his lungs or he would have told her to stop this torture now…or never.

She wrapped her arms around him, slipped her hands beneath the waistband of his trousers and dug her nails into his hips as she began to suckle, first on one nipple and then the other.

When he felt the scrape of her teeth, Chance groaned. What was she doing to him? He'd desired her before. And the strength of that desire had made him reckless and rough. But what she was doing to him now made him weak. No other woman had made him feel this way. Fear mixed with a need so deep that he felt paralyzed.

"You still have too many clothes on," she murmured.

In the wall of mirrors, he watched her move around him. Her tongue stroked lightly on the skin at the back of his neck, then trailed a damp path down his spine. His skin felt icy and hot at the same time. He couldn't think, could barely breathe as he watched her strip him of his belt and send his trousers to the floor. Next she removed his briefs. Then she moved around so that she was facing him again.

More than anything he wanted to grab her, pull her to the floor and bury himself in her. But his arms still felt heavy, and he wasn't sure that he could raise them.

"Watch," she said. "I'm going to touch you now."

He was helpless to do anything else as she closed both of her hands around him. Her fingers were hot, and she was doing something magical, twisting gently with one hand at the base of his penis as she pulled with the other.

"I'm going to make you come," she said.

He wanted to crush her to him. He wanted to feel her beneath him on the floor. But he couldn't take his eyes off what she was doing to him in the mirror. The steady movement of her hands and the incredible waves of pleasure she was bringing him.

She moved closer to him then until her lips were brushing his. "You can kiss me now. Why don't you kiss me while you're coming?"

Whether it was her words or the fact that she kissed him, Chance felt strength and power return to his arms. He gripped the front of her dress and ripped it down the center. Then she was beneath him on the floor.

They rolled as one, mouth to mouth, body to body. Triumphant, Natalie gave herself over to Chance and to the needs that consumed her. This was what she'd wanted from him—this consuming hunger. She could feel the power of it as his hands raced over her, molding, pressing, bruising. She rolled on top of him and devoured. His skin tasted darker and more dangerous now. But she only got a sample before she was crushed beneath him again.

And then he was poised above her.

"Look at me while I take you."

She stared into his eyes and saw herself. *I need you.* The words pulsed through her as he drove himself into her. And she gave herself over to the madness.

CHANCE WINCED as he stepped beneath the cold spray of the shower. He was hoping it would clear his mind of the woman he'd just spent the night with. He needed to think.

Just who the hell was she?

As he lathered his shoulders and arms with soap, Chance considered that very fascinating question. The blonde with the sky-blue eyes was definitely Natalie

Gibbs but in her new persona, she was different. "Rachel" was more playful, more inventive—he frowned, searching for the right word—more free.

It wasn't that one woman was any sexier than the other. They were simply two thoroughly delightful sides of Natalie Gibbs, a woman he'd wanted with a desperation that had taken him to the limits of his control—and beyond.

Still, the differences between Natalie and "Rachel" fascinated him. Detective Gibbs had the cool head and the detachment of a cop. He'd admired that from the first time they'd met. And even in the way she made love, she was focused. "Rachel" seemed more impulsive. She had a talent for absorbing herself entirely in the moment. Damned if she hadn't tempted him into doing the same. In fact, he'd been so absorbed in her that instead of coming up with a plan to convince her to join him on his Florida job, he'd just given himself over to exploring the pleasure they could bring to each other.

The whole night had been a battle, and Chance still wasn't sure who'd won. He could vividly recall the way her hands had torn at his clothes and his had torn at hers, the way he'd finally dragged her to the floor and she'd wrestled him across it.

He wondered if he would ever forget the way her body had bucked and shuddered beneath his, or the way she'd cried out his name as they'd both drowned in pleasure. Each time when they'd finished with each other, they should have been content. But they hadn't been. Their appetites had been insatiable.

Never had the need to possess a woman been so intense. It should have scared him. He should have wanted to get out of there—and fast. On some level, he was sure that he did. But overriding that fear was the determination to have Natalie Gibbs with him when he went to Brancotti's estate.

Turning around, he let the cold water slap him in the face. The night was over. He had to get it out of his head and decide how to approach her about the Florida job.

Would she admit to him this morning that she was Natalie Gibbs, or would she continue to pretend that she was Rachel Cade? That was the question.

It might be fun to have them both along on the Florida job. But having fun wasn't the issue. Catching his old childhood nemesis was. He couldn't allow himself to jeopardize that.

After stepping out of the shower, Chance grabbed a towel and rubbed himself dry. The night was over. If Natalie didn't put an end to the masquerade, he would. The situation might be a little difficult at first—especially if she didn't want to be unmasked. But Natalie, the cop, was someone he knew how to deal with because they were a great deal alike.

Still, he thought with a smile, he was going to miss Rachel.

NATALIE SURFACED SLOWLY, her senses awakening one at a time. Rain—the steady sound of it lulled her. Keeping her eyes closed, she let herself drift, savoring the protection of the warm cocoon she was still wrapped in. This was one of her favorite parts of the day, the brief span of time in the morning before her alarm rang when she could feel the sunlight splashing across her bed, see the lightness of it beyond her eyelids and still not have to face it.

Burrowing more deeply into her pillow, she drew in a deep breath. Something was different. For a moment she couldn't put a name to it. How could she feel sunshine and hear the soft, steady fall of rain at the same time? Even as the question formed in her mind, she realized it wasn't the scent of her vanilla candle she smelled. It was…Chance.

Opening her eyes, she sat up as everything came flooding back into her mind. A quick glance around the room told her that she hadn't dreamed the night she'd just spent with Chance Mitchell. She was in a suite at the Meridian, and the rain that had lulled her was the sound of the shower.

When it had stopped, she pushed hair out of her face and felt a little flutter of panic. At any moment Chance could step into the room.

And then what?

The second flutter of panic was strong enough to have her throwing back the covers and grabbing one of the hotel robes. As she was tying the belt, she caught sight of herself in the mirror and dropped her hands. She wasn't Natalie Gibbs. Lifting a hand, she toyed with the ends of her hair. She was Rachel Cade. Natalie might have concerned herself with morning-after etiquette, but Rachel Cade didn't.

A smile curved her lips. After living in Rachel's skin for one long glorious night, Natalie knew that her alter ego didn't concern herself with much of anything but the pursuit of pleasure.

Raising her arms over her head, she stretched. Each little twinge of muscle brought back images and sensations from the night she'd just spent with Chance Mitchell.

He *had* kissed her—finally. And the man had an incredible mouth. She ran her fingers over her lips and sighed. Nothing had ever come close to what she'd felt or what she'd done during the two nights she'd spent with Chance Mitchell. Natalie might have worried about that. But Rachel was already wondering about stretching the experience into another day at least— and perhaps a night.

Natalie laughed. She was going to have to thank Sierra for her suggestion. Sex was a lot more fun when you didn't have to bring your personal baggage along.

A buzzer sounded at the door of the room and she heard a muffled voice say, "Room service."

When she opened the door, the waiter rolled a cart in and positioned it near a window that offered a view of the Mall.

"Rolls and glassware are on the lower shelf. Will there be anything else, ma'am?"

Natalie waved a dismissive hand, but she couldn't take her eyes off the spread that the waiter had delivered. Four white plates with silver covers were arranged on a cheery yellow cloth and in the center stood a pitcher of orange juice, a thermal container of coffee and a champagne bottle in a silver bucket.

A funny little feeling moved through her as she ran a finger over a single yellow rose that lay on one napkin. This kind of care wasn't something she'd come to expect from a man.

She peeked under one silver lid and saw crisp bacon and plump sausages.

"I didn't know what you'd like, so I ordered a bit of everything."

Natalie turned to see Chance walk into the room. He was wearing trousers, but not his shirt. His feet were bare, his hair still damp from the shower. Her throat went dry. Incredibly, she wanted him all over again.

"I'd like *you*," she said.

THE VOICE, the look she was giving him told Chance it was still Rachel he was dealing with, and if she continued to look at him in that way, the breakfast he'd ordered was going to get very cold.

Business, Chance reminded himself. *Keep it light.* "I thought it might be nice if we shared a meal—since we never got around to eating last night. That way we can talk and get to know one another."

She laughed. "So we have a night of wild, sweaty sex and then we have a date?"

It occurred to him that he'd never had a date with Natalie in either of her personas. "Something like that. I'd like to get to know you."

It was nothing less than the truth. In spite of his resolution to end the game she was playing, he was still intrigued by this side of Natalie. What could it hurt to delay the unmasking until after breakfast?

Natalie lifted one of the silver covers at random, then settled herself into a chair. "An omelet. I guess I could use the protein for energy."

It was his turn to laugh as he took the seat across

from her. Oh, it was definitely Rachel he was dealing with. He was going to miss her. "I was beginning to think you had an unending supply."

She sliced into the eggs. "Well, we could certainly test your theory."

Chance concentrated on the practical matter of lifting silver covers until he found what he was looking for. Then he scooped yogurt into a bowl and added fresh fruit and a little wheat germ.

"I'm sorry," she said.

He glanced up startled. "What for?"

"That." She pointed to his bowl of yogurt. "You must have ordered that for me. Here." She pushed her plate toward him. "Have some of the omelet. It's delicious."

"Thanks, but this is what I eat every day."

"You're kidding."

The horrified expression on her face made him smile. "I like to be careful about what I put into my body."

"And here I'd pegged you for a risk-taker." She met his eyes. "But I guess you're doing something right. You've got a great body."

She was making it hard to stick to the date plan. "What do you usually eat for breakfast?"

She shrugged as she lifted another forkful of eggs. "I'm a cop, so you get one guess."

"Donuts?"

She pointed a fork at him. "You got it. I prefer them day old so I can dunk them in the dreadful coffee they serve at the station."

Chance's eyes narrowed. "So…you're a cop like your cousin Natalie?"

As she set her cup down, some of the coffee spilled onto the saucer. "Yes. Fort Lauderdale."

For a few moments, she busied herself with eating, and Chance wondered if admitting to being a cop had been a slipup. Perhaps, now was the time to tell her that he knew who she was. He could reach over, take her hand and say, "Natalie, I know."

But once he did that, would "Rachel" disappear? "Do you like being a cop?"

"Sure." This time when her eyes met his he saw a trace of amusement. "Is this the part where we exchange bios?"

Chance shrugged as he set down his spoon. "Standard first date talk. You interest me, Rachel Cade. Ever do any undercover work on the job?"

She hesitated only an instant. "Some. You should see me in my hooker clothes."

A vivid image filled Chance's mind, but he shoved it away. "I've heard your cousin Natalie is good with locks. Any chance that you're good with them, too?"

Her eyes narrowed slightly. "Anything Nat can do, I can do better. You know, this is beginning to sound like a job interview."

Chance couldn't help thinking that Rachel's mind was every bit as sharp as her "cousin's." "How long are you going to be visiting your cousins?"

"I'm not sure." She lifted her cup and drained it. Then she sent him a provocative smile. "Why do you ask?"

Because at some point in their conversation, Chance had scratched his original game plan and come up with a new one. He wasn't at all ready to lose Rachel Cade yet. He wanted her in Florida with him. His head might tell him that he was taking a dangerous risk by not ending Natalie's masquerade right now, but something much closer to the bone was telling him that he was going to need both women to catch Brancotti. "I've got a little proposition to make you and it will involve about a week of your time."

She reached over and ran a finger down the back of his hand. "Sounds perfect. Especially, if it's anything like the proposition I made you last night...."

Chance shook his head. "It's more of a job offer, and it's dangerous." He saw something flicker in her eyes, just once. Surprise or something else? "You'll have to wear a disguise."

She said nothing, but her expression had stilled and the woman studying him now was Detective Natalie Gibbs through and through.

"I was thinking of asking your cousin Natalie. I need someone who's good at disguise and it wouldn't hurt at all if you could break into a safe. If you're interested, I think we could work very well together."

She said nothing at all, but he could almost hear the wheels turning in her head. Chance felt a little sinking sensation in his stomach. Would she tell him that she was really Natalie? With the seconds ticking away, he watched her closely. If there was any struggle going on inside of her, he saw no evidence of it. Oh, this was the cool, sharp detective all right. But he couldn't help remembering the impulsive and incredibly responsive woman he'd spent the night with. How many other facets were there to Natalie Gibbs?

Finally, she said, "I might be interested. Tell me what it involves."

Leaning forward, Chance did just that. He explained everything just as he had to Tracker—the missing Ferrante diamond, its resurfacing and the upcoming auction for a select group of invited guests. Then he told her about the cover. They would go in as a billionaire software nerd and his current piece of arm candy. The only things he left out were Venetia Gaston's death and his personal relationship to Brancotti.

"Brancotti's estate is in South Florida. Have you heard of him?"

Natalie shook her head. "We wouldn't if he keeps himself as clean as you say he does."

Smooth, Chance thought. But of course, she wouldn't lie unless she had to. No one who had lived undercover and had to tell lies for long periods of time ever told more than necessary.

"What do you say?" Chance asked.

YES. NATALIE HAD to bite down hard on the inside of her cheek to keep from saying the word out loud. As much as the "Rachel" part of her wanted to agree, she knew that she had to think. More than that, she needed to make a few phone calls and find out more about this Brancotti. She couldn't just up and run off to Florida and pretend to be some high-tech billionaire's arm candy. Could she?

Of course not. She never acted on impulse. Oh, she took risks, certainly. But she always weighed her options, ascertained the consequences and made plans accordingly.

But she was so tempted to throw caution to the wind and say yes. Chance was offering her just the kind of assignment she'd always dreamed of. She could use her talents, and she would be working with one of the best men in his field.

She lifted the pot and refilled her cup. There were other things to consider. There had to be. For one thing, he thought she was Rachel Cade. She should tell him right now about the trick she'd pulled on him. But if she did, would he become annoyed and withdraw his offer?

Plus, she wasn't at all sure that she wanted to give up being Rachel Cade.

The voice came then, pushing past the fears and doubts skulking around in her mind like a shadowy thief. *"Trust in your talents."*

Chance chose that moment to take her hand in his and raise it to his lips. "What do you say, Rachel?"

It was Natalie who was dithering, and she knew in an instant what Rachel would say.

"What time do we leave?"

SHE HAD TO BE CRAZY, Natalie thought as she lifted the ten-pound weights that Chance had given her. He selected heavier ones for himself, then turned to face her.

"Do what I do," he said as he raised his arms until they were level with his shoulders, held for a count of five and then lowered them.

She did. Although she'd told him that she was in good shape, he'd insisted on putting her to the test. The moment that she'd agreed to go with him to Florida, he'd told her that they were going to take a five-mile run through Rock Creek Park. He'd even bought her some shoes and workout clothes in one of the hotel's gift shops.

When she'd asked why he was testing her, he'd merely said that he needed to make sure she could keep up with him if they had to make a run for it. The run had lasted well beyond five miles. After forty minutes she was still matching him stride for stride, and he'd been the one to call it quits.

Now they were using the hotel gym. It was located on the lobby level, and offered weight machines, treadmills, free weights and a large pool that started indoors and ended outside. Four glass walls made the room about as private as a fishbowl.

Lifting the weights to her shoulders, she began to follow Chance's lead through a combination of lunges and squats. When he finally set down his weights and took hers, he said, "You're good."

Her brows shot up. "I'm a cop, remember."

"Not all cops stay in shape." Then turning, he led the way to a mat. "Let's see what you can do in hand-to-hand combat."

For a moment she stared at him. "You're serious?"

He smiled at her. "Unless you think you can't take me."

Unable to resist the challenge, she stepped onto the mat and began to circle slowly. He knew what buttons to push. She'd have to remember that and push a few of her own. He was bigger than she was and stronger. On the job when she'd had to use physical force, she'd always been able to play the looks-like-a-fragile-woman card. That wouldn't work here. So her best option was distraction.

Keeping her eyes on his, she said, "What's next? Target practice?"

He laughed, and she very nearly allowed herself to be distracted by the sound as she moved in and hooked her foot behind his. Once she had him off balance, she aimed her elbow at his stomach. An instant before it connected, she found her arms pinned to her side and before she could blink, she was lying beneath him, facedown on the mat.

While she struggled for a breath, she was vaguely aware of applause. But she was much more aware of Chance's body pressing hers into the mat, of his voice in her ear. "You'll have to work on your eyes. They give you away."

She would work on that, she vowed as she got to her feet.

This time she let him make the move, and she blocked it.

"Good," he said. "Now try this one."

He moved fast as a snake, but she moved faster. He didn't talk after that, and neither did she. She wasn't even sure how much time had passed as he made one move after another and she attempted to block them. She lost count of how often she ended up pinned to the floor. But each time, he helped her to her feet and taught her the countermove that would have stopped him.

He was very good, better than any martial arts instructor she'd ever trained under. But she would have bitten her tongue out rather than tell him. Nor was she about to tell him that she'd never before responded to martial arts instruction like it was foreplay. Her mind might be calculating countermoves, but her body had become very sensitized to his touch. In the course of their workout, his forearms had brushed against her breasts. His hands had gripped her calves, her thighs, her hips. Twice when they'd rolled on the floor his leg had been between her thighs. When he finally called it quits and grinned at her, in spite of her annoyance, she wanted to jump him.

If there hadn't been an audience with their noses pressed against the glass walls surrounding them, she might have. Instead, she smiled at him, shook his hand. As they walked together toward the shower rooms, she bided her time. When he was least expecting it, she gave him a quick shove into the pool.

Then with the applause of the spectators in her ears, she waited until he surfaced and grinned down at him. "Thanks for the tip about the eyes."

"Anytime," he said as he gripped the side of the pool. "I don't suppose you want to give me a hand out of the pool."

She grinned down at him. "Do I have the word Sucker written on my forehead?" Then she turned and walked away.

CARLO BRANCOTTI sat in his office, looking over the file that Lisa had just handed him. Sun streamed through the open French doors and a breeze from the ocean played with the wind chimes on the patio. When he finished reading Lisa's report, he glanced up. "So— which one of these would a clever insurance investigator choose to impersonate?"

"I don't know. I wasn't able to eliminate any of them."

Carlo studied her for a moment. Lisa was a very cautious woman. He paid her to be just that. "Take an educated guess. If you wanted to trap Carlo Brancotti, which one of these people would you attempt to impersonate?"

She thought for a moment. "I'd choose Steven Bradford. But you don't pay me for guessing."

"Why Bradford?"

"I suppose because he's so squeaky clean. He's never entered this kind of a market before. Plus, he avoids the press. The only picture I was able to come up with was from his college days. If Interpol wanted to slip someone in, we'd be hard-pressed to see through the disguise."

It wasn't Interpol he was worried about. Carlo studied the picture of a thin young man with long, brownish-blond hair. Bradford would be twelve years older now, a man instead of a boy. The body would have filled out, the hairstyle changed.

"Good choice," he murmured. Then he glanced at the photos of Steven Bradford's current girlfriend.

She hadn't been a model long. The one layout that Lisa had come up with featured a tall blonde modeling a bathing suit while playing volleyball. She was wearing sunglasses in each picture. He picked one up and studied it more closely. Steven Bradford was a lucky man. "What about the woman? This..." he paused to find the name, "Calli? The government doesn't always send a male agent."

Lisa frowned. "But you won't invite her to the actual auction. She won't have access to the diamond."

True. Still, he wasn't going to dismiss the possibility that the model known only as Calli wasn't as harmless as she appeared. He was going to enjoy getting to know her better when she arrived. He picked up the next picture. "What about Armand Genovese?"

"He would be my second choice. He's wearing a hat and sunglasses in every picture, so we can't be sure what he looks like either. Also this is his first venture into the black market."

Now Carlo smiled. "Only because he has other sources for stolen art and jewels. Ones that don't always require top dollar."

"True. Which makes it a little surprising for him to contact you. Perhaps because of his methods of acquisition he's made a deal with the government."

"Good point." This was precisely why he paid Lisa McGill a very good salary. She had a razor-sharp mind as well as a knack for computers and research.

For the first time since she'd come into the room, Lisa relaxed slightly. "Thank you, sir."

Carlo turned his attention to the third photo. When it had been taken, Risa Manwaring had been the toast of Hollywood. That had been at least twenty-five years ago. "And why might a very clever insurance agent choose to impersonate Risa Manwaring?"

"Because once she married that British lord, she shunned the press, so no telling what she looks like now. And as you said yourself, the government doesn't always send a male agent."

"True. Good work, Lisa," Carlo said as he slipped the file into a drawer and locked it.

"Thank you, sir."

"When Bradford arrives, we'll put him in the Venetian room. That way we can keep very close tabs on him. Signore Genovese will stay in the Tuscan room, and Ms. Manwaring in the Neopolitan room. Make sure that all three rooms are wired and that the security cameras in the walls are well hidden."

"I'll see to it myself, sir."

When Lisa left the room, Carlo rose from his desk and turned to the painting that hung behind him. After moving it aside, he opened his safe and took out two velvet pouches. One was red and the other was black. After setting them on his desk, he removed a diamond from each pouch, then carried them out through the French doors to his patio. It was early, not yet eight o'clock, but the sun was pouring directly into the courtyard. It shot light into both stones and the facets in each captured that light and seemed to glow from within.

Both were a rare shade of canary-yellow, and only one of them was real—the Ferrante diamond. The other was a very carefully crafted fake. Only a skilled gemologist would be able to tell the difference.

Carlo smiled as he looked down at them. He would use them both to set a trap for "Chance Mitchell." There was nothing that he enjoyed more than a game of cat and mouse with a worthy opponent.

Too bad that he would have to end the game for good this time.

7

By THE TIME Natalie arrived at the Blue Pepper, second thoughts were attacking with a vengeance. Not that the "Rachel Cade" part of her was having any. No, it was good old Natalie who'd called her sisters for an emergency meeting. She'd told Chance she had to talk to her "cousins" and inform them of her change in plans.

The restaurant was crowded. And the number of patrons, more than the quick glance she gave her watch, told her that she was running more than half an hour late. And she was never late. At least Natalie wasn't ever late. Plus, she was exhausted. Both conditions, she blamed completely on Chance Mitchell.

During a long, grueling day of cramming, shopping and packing, she'd discovered a whole new side to the man—one that made her think of Simon LaGree. Not in a million years would she have suspected that the laid-back man she'd known as Chance Mitchell would turn into such a taskmaster.

The run in Rock Creek Park and the workout had just been the beginning. When she'd passed those little tests, he'd dragged her back to his room at the Meridian to study. He hadn't been satisfied until she'd known everything there was to know about Carlo Brancotti.

He'd even quizzed her. Of course, she'd passed. She prided herself on her sharp memory.

Brancotti wasn't the only name he'd ever used. There were at least half a dozen other aliases, and the man hadn't limited his dealings to art and jewels. Over the years, he'd trafficked in just about every black market commodity he could lay his hands on, including drugs and arms. Brancotti's trademark as a jewel thief was leaving a high quality fake jewel in place of the real one, and usually by the time the theft was discovered the trail was cold.

By the end of the cramming session, the cop part of her had known that she hadn't made a mistake in agreeing to Chance's proposition.

It was the feminine part of her that was having second thoughts. Pushing past the crowd clustered around the hostess station, she scanned the restaurant and spotted her sisters seated at a small table on the upper level. They were looking in her direction, but when she waved, they didn't seem to see her.

Of course, they were looking for Rachel Cade. And she wasn't Rachel anymore. Thanks to Chance Mitchell, she'd been transformed into "Calli," a wannabe supermodel who'd been cohabiting with software billionaire Steven Bradford for the past six months.

"Welcome to the Blue Pepper."

Natalie glanced down to see that Rad had suddenly appeared in her path. "Hi." Though she smiled at him, he didn't grab her hands or kiss the air near her cheeks. The disguise must be working with him, too. But then he wasn't looking at her face. His eyes were riveted on the skinny tank top she was wearing.

"Oh my, oh my, oh my." He pressed a hand to his heart as he stepped back to run his eyes down her. "Oh my, oh my, oh my."

Several people turned to stare, and Natalie glanced down, praying that everything about the skimpy outfit she was wearing was still in place. Both the pink shorts and top were cut high, leaving plenty of leg and stomach bare. She tugged the edge of the shorts down a bit, hoping there wasn't anything showing that might get her ticketed for indecent exposure.

"What's wrong?" she asked.

"Nothing. You are perfection! The hair, the shoes. And that color is soooooo you!" Rad clapped his hands together. "I have a friend who should be wearing this color. I've told her over and over to think pink."

As Rad began to circle her, she caught a glimpse of herself in one of the mirrored columns that flanked the bar.

She had to hand it to Chance. It was the perfect outfit for her new alter ego. The hair, the earrings that fell to just above her shoulders, even the ankle-breaking sandals suited "Calli" to a *T,* and the whole package together sent out a promise of hot, steamy sex.

Rad had completed his circle, and he was facing her now. "*Love* the hair! Where did you get that cut?"

Beginning to enjoy herself, Natalie tucked a curl behind her ear as she leaned down to whisper. "Arturo at the Meridian."

"He is an artist!"

"Thanks. I'm looking for the Gibbs sisters."

"Wonderful! Then you'll get to meet my friend, Detective Natalie. She's not here yet," he said as he began to cut a path through the crowd for her. "You must tell her about Arturo."

Natalie recalled that Chance had slipped Arturo an enormously large tip to layer her hair and pile on the products until it looked like she'd just got out of bed with a man. But she hadn't gotten a chance to see if she could achieve the look naturally by doing just that. Chance, the taskmaster, hadn't made a move on her since she'd agreed to work with him on the Brancotti job.

There hadn't been much time, of course. Still, the change in him had started her thinking. Had he gotten his fill of Rachel Cade in one night just as he seemed to have gotten his fill of Natalie?

Would the same fate await Calli?

As they reached the stairs, she shot a quick look over her shoulder and caught her reflection again in the mirror. Calli might have something to say about that. Rachel definitely would. Perhaps the two women would have to tag-team him. A quick laugh bubbled up at the direction her thoughts had taken. On her own, she would never have come up with that idea. She was beginning to enjoy the different persons she was discovering within herself.

Rad stopped at the top of the short flight of stairs and pointed in the direction of her sisters. Pushing all thoughts of Chance out of her mind, Natalie made her way to the table.

"Do you mind if I join you?" she asked.

"Sorry," Sierra said, glancing up at her.

"We're waiting for our sister," Rory explained.

"She won't mind," Natalie said as she settled herself in the empty chair.

"Now, wait just a minute," Rory began. "You can't just…"

"Wait." Sierra cut off her sister by squeezing her hand. In the space of five beats, Natalie saw the recognition seep into her youngest sister's eyes.

Three seconds later, Rory said, "Who in the hell are you supposed to be?"

"The name is Calli, and I'm a wannabe supermodel."

"Okay," Rory said, intrigued now. "I can buy that. The question is *why?*"

Natalie sighed and signaled a waiter. "It's a long story, and I need a drink."

"What'll it be, ladies?"

"A martini, dry with an olive," Natalie said.

"Make that three," Rory said not taking her eyes off of Natalie. "And we'll have the appetizer sampler." The moment the waiter hurried off, she said, "Whatever the story is, I vote you wear that outfit every time we come here. We've never gotten service this fast before."

"What I want to know is what happened to our dear cousin Rachel?" Sierra asked. "Didn't the disguise work?"

"Oh, it worked. Maybe too well." Then Natalie leaned forward and told them everything, pausing only when the waiter served their drinks. Once she'd finished, Rory drained the last of her martini and said, "You were getting bored with your job. This man has offered you the kind of assignment you've always secretly dreamed of having. On top of all that, you're attracted to him. What's the problem?"

Natalie shifted her gaze from Rory to Sierra.

Sierra shook her head. "Don't look at me. I think Rory summed the situation up nicely. Unless you don't think you can pull it off."

Natalie shook her head. "The job isn't the problem. I can do it. It's Chance. He's the problem."

"So?" Sierra asked. "Is he going to be any less of a problem if you change your mind and tell him Rachel doesn't want to turn herself into Calli and fly to Florida tomorrow?"

Natalie thought for a minute. "No, but…"

"You'll only regret it if you let this opportunity slip by," Sierra said.

"And you won't just be saying goodbye to the job. You'll be kissing off the guy, too," Rory pointed out. "Are you ready to do that yet?"

Natalie sipped her martini, then set her glass down. That was the real problem. She wasn't ready to cut Chance adrift. Not yet.

"I thought spending another night with him would get him out of my system," she said.

"That's one of the problems with our society," Sierra said. "We want quick fixes, and sometimes that's just not possible."

Narrowing her eyes, Natalie glanced from to Sierra to Rory. "I wanted the two of you to talk some sense into me."

Rory shot her a bland look. "I thought that's exactly what we were doing."

"We think you ought to go," Sierra said.

Natalie ran her finger around the rim of the martini she'd hardly touched. "I should probably tell him that I'm Natalie."

"Why? It's Rachel he invited along," Sierra pointed out.

Rory grinned at her. "Do you really want to go back to being Natalie yet?"

"No." She wasn't ready to give up being Rachel Cade yet. "But I've never tried to be two people at once before."

Rory rolled her eyes. "You can't have forgotten that Halloween when you were Wonder Woman and you kept slipping away from us so you could reappear and terrorize us as Jason from *Friday the Thirteenth.* You did it three times before we figured out it was just you."

Natalie laughed. "I had forgotten that. Still, this is a little different."

"Do you still want Chance Mitchell?" Sierra asked.

"Yes, but…"

"That's Natalie talking," Sierra pointed out. "How does Rachel feel about it?"

Natalie grimaced. "She's the one who said 'yes.'"

"What about Calli?" Rory asked.

"*She's* got her bags packed."

"There you go," Rory said. "Two to one—they've outvoted you."

Sierra reached over to take her hand. "Calli and Rachel are parts of you. Maybe it's time you trusted them."

Grinning, Rory lifted her glass in a toast. "To quote Harry, 'trust in your talents.'"

Sierra smiled and raised her glass. "'Risk anything it takes.'"

CHANCE STRODE into the bedroom and checked the suitcases for the third time since Natalie had left. The designer name luggage looked well used. Brancotti would notice that. He was a man who noticed everything. Not even a small detail would escape him. And new luggage would give rise to questions.

That had been the reason that he'd urged Natalie to pack some of Rachel's clothes as well as the new things they'd purchased for "Calli." He'd insisted on stopping by Natalie's place where "Rachel" was staying so she could collect her belongings. Flipping open the top of one of the smaller pieces, Chance fingered a lace camisole in a shade of icy pink. He'd often wondered what Detective Natalie Gibbs had worn beneath those tailored suits. In his mind, he'd pictured the stereotypical black lace, but for some odd reason, he found the pale pastel shade even more alluring. Of course, he'd known that Natalie had her vulnerable side. What he hadn't known was that it would appeal to him just as much as her strength did.

When he caught himself reaching for Rachel's cosmetic bag, he stopped himself. He'd already checked it and assured himself that it contained a mix of new and old makeup—just as any woman's would. The only question he wanted in Brancotti's mind was how much Steven Bradford would pay for the Ferrante—the diamond that had already caused the death of a fellow agent.

For a moment, he let himself think of Venetia Gaston, the woman who'd been his partner during his last encounter with the man who now called himself Carlo Brancotti. For two years, he'd blamed himself for Venetia's death. He'd set up the meet, and it should have gone smoothly. Carlo was to bring the diamond he'd just stolen and Venetia was to turn over the money. Then Interpol would move in. But Venetia had never reached the spot where the exchange was to take place. Carlo had intercepted her somehow. When they'd found her body, the money had been gone, and she'd had a fake diamond in her purse.

Chance firmly pushed the image of Venetia out of his mind. Dwelling on a past mistake was not going to help him now. He drew his thoughts back to the present and lifted a skinny little tank top that he'd had "Calli" model for him earlier in the day. This time he wasn't taking any chances. He was going to face his old nemesis himself, and he was taking someone in with him that Brancotti would have no way of knowing. Chance's lips curved slightly. How could Brancotti know that the sexy woman known as Calli was also a tough cop who was equally adept at handling a gun and opening safes?

Chance dropped the tank top and closed the suitcase. The suite had suddenly seemed empty when she'd walked out. Her request to meet with her "cousins" had surprised him, but it had made sense. Of course, she would want to let her sisters know that she was leaving town. But what if she had second thoughts? How could he handle them if he wasn't there?

Turning, he strode back into the living room of the suite. He'd just have to handle them when she got back. He wasn't going to Florida without Natalie Gibbs. The file he'd shown her that afternoon was still spread out on the coffee table. He doubted she was aware of it, but when she worked she was all police detective. The intensity of her concentration and the strength of her endurance—both were qualities he'd come to admire throughout the long and grueling day he'd put her through.

She hadn't once flinched or complained. And not so much as by a twitch of a muscle had she let it be known that anything in his old enemy's file had shocked her. She'd looked up from it once to say, "You lost your partner?"

"Yes," he'd said. She deserved to know the truth. "Brancotti killed her."

"I'm sorry." Then she'd gone back to reading the rest of the file. When she'd finished and met his eyes, there'd been the look of a warrior on her face.

Recalling it now, he felt more reassured than he'd been since she'd left. The woman who'd read that file wouldn't back out on him. She wanted to bring Brancotti to justice almost as much as he did. Isn't that why he'd wanted her with him in the first place?

Or at least partly the reason, he thought as his gaze moved to the foyer, one of the many places in the suite where they'd succumbed to their desires the night before. How many times during the day had he wanted to make love to her again? Hell, he'd nearly pulled her into the woods at Rock Creek Park and taken her there. The truth was he wanted Natalie/Rachel/Calli—all of the women who made up Natalie Gibbs—with an intensity that had him being…cautious. No woman had even made him cautious before.

When the doorbell rang, Chance strode forward to

answer it. But it wasn't Natalie he found on the other side. It was Tracker and Lucas, carrying a brown bag.

"Are we interrupting anything?" Lucas asked.

"No." Chance hoped that he was hiding his disappointment as he stepped back from the door.

"We thought you might be busy with that blonde you left Sophie's party with." Tracker removed a six-pack of imported beer from the bag.

"'Beware of Greeks bearing gifts,'" Chance quoted as he took the one Tracker offered to him. "What's up?"

"Tracker is worried about you," Lucas said.

Chance raised his brows. "I'm touched."

"I've been doing a little digging on Brancotti, alias Phillipe Sagan, alias 'Damien.' The two of you go back a long way."

Chance didn't even let a flicker of surprise show. He'd known that Tracker was about the best there was when it came to running background checks, but he hadn't expected him to unearth the "Damien" alias. Still, there was no way he could have traced Damien back to that orphanage. "I've been tracking him for a long time."

"And you lost your partner in Rome two years ago," Tracker said.

"Yes, I did."

"Besides being dangerous, this man has the reputation of being very smart." Tracker raised a hand when Chance opened his mouth to give his opinion. "Let me finish. Lucas and I will concede that you're a very smart man, too. The thing is you nearly had Brancotti for stealing this diamond two years ago. He's not a man who'll forget that. Put yourself in his place. There's a good chance that he took the time to find out exactly who was on his trail then, and that he's kept tabs on you. He could be expecting you."

Chance took a swallow of his beer. "I'm sure he is."

"It could be a trap," Lucas said.

Chance met his old friend's eyes. "It could be. But I wouldn't be where I am today if I ran every time I suspected a trap."

Lucas glanced at Tracker. "I told you we wouldn't talk him out of it."

"Relax," Chance said. "There's no way he can suspect my cover. We've built it very carefully. Both Steven Bradford and his current love interest have agreed to go into seclusion until this is over. Their private plane will arrive here tomorrow morning. They will be whisked off in a hired limousine and delivered here to this suite where they will stay until the job is done. Steven is shy of the press. I won't have any trouble passing for him."

"I want to go in as your bodyguard," Tracker said. "Someone who hides from the press as much as Bradford does would be eccentric enough to insist on a personal bodyguard."

Chance shook his head. "The invitation was very specific. One guest. If Bradford tries to bring anyone besides his girlfriend at this point, it could mean he'll be refused admittance to the estate, and I won't risk that. Besides, Natalie Gibbs is perfectly qualified to be my bodyguard."

Tracker and Lucas exchanged looks again.

"You convinced Natalie Gibbs to be your partner then?" Tracker asked.

Chance hesitated for only a second, then cursed himself for it. "Yes." He knew that both of his friends were studying him more closely now. In another minute they'd demand to know the whole story.

"Natalie never did show up for Sophie's party, and you left with a blonde," Tracker pointed out.

"It's a long story," Chance said.

Tracker passed a beer to Lucas and took one for himself. "If we're your backup and rescue team, we deserve to be filled in."

Since he couldn't argue with that, Chance took another drink of his beer and then laid it out for them. By the time he was finished, both men were frowning and regarding him intently.

"So she doesn't know that you know she's really Natalie Gibbs?" Tracker asked.

"Right," Chance said.

"Why the masquerade in the first place?" Lucas asked.

"I couldn't ask without letting her know I saw through the disguise," Chance said.

"Right," Tracker said. "That much makes sense. What doesn't make sense is why you didn't inform her that you knew who she really was."

Chance's brows shot up. "Hey, I didn't see through her disguise at first. Neither did the two of you." He'd like to think that he would have seen through it even if he hadn't overheard her sisters talking. "Even though I quickly realized it was Natalie, that doesn't change the fact that a very sexy and attractive blonde made a play for me. By the time my brain was functioning again, things had gotten…complicated. I wanted Natalie on this job with me for a number of reasons. My chances were slim to none if I got her pissed at me for not fessing up that I'd known it was her almost from the get-go."

Lucas's grin spread slowly. "In other words, you made your bed, and now you have to lie in it."

"Yeah." Chance sighed. "Something like that."

Tracker took a sip of his beer and then asked, "Is she aware of the dangers?"

"She's read the file. She knows about my last partner. And she knows what kind of man Brancotti is."

"Okay, so both of you are aware that you're dealing with a very nasty guy. Have you considered the possibility that there's someone on the inside of the insurance business who's on Brancotti's payroll?" Tracker asked.

Chance met his friend's eyes steadily. "I've had two years to think about how he got away with the diamond the last time. He had to have been getting inside information to steal the diamond in the first place. That's why I insisted that no one could know the route that Venetia was taking that day except me."

Tracker frowned. "And Venetia. You think she was the traitor?"

"I've given it some consideration. Carlo's quite a ladies' man. Perhaps he used her, then killed her because she'd served her purpose and he didn't want to share. This time I'm working on my own. No one at the insurance office knows I'm going in as Bradford. I haven't even told them that the Ferrante diamond has resurfaced."

"I told you he'd be on top of it," Lucas said, then glanced at Chance. "Tracker here's a real worrywart."

"Humor me," Tracker said as he passed a slip of paper to Chance. "That's my private cell phone number. You're the only person who can call me on it. As long as you're on that estate, I'll be close by."

Chance glanced at it, memorized it and handed it back.

"You better make sure that Natalie memorizes it, too," Lucas said, "just in case."

"Done," Chance said.

Tracker leaned back and for the first time since he'd entered the room, he smiled. "One other thing."

"Yeah?"

"What happens when Rachel finds out that you've known all along she's really Natalie?" Tracker asked.

"I'll handle it," Chance said. And he wished to hell that he felt as confident as he sounded.

8

"YOU'RE SURE you've got it?" Chance asked as the limousine pulled away from the Meridian. There wasn't even a hint of the sun in the eastern sky, and the streetlights they passed offered only intermittent illumination in the car.

Natalie gave him a sharp salute. "Aye-aye, sir. From the time we step on the plane we are no longer Chance Mitchell and Rachel Cade. We are Steven Bradford who's just made another million or two this morning and his new best friend, Calli." She tilted her head to one side. "You really think Brancotti might have Steven Bradford's plane bugged?"

"It's been sitting on the runway since yesterday evening. I'm banking on it."

Her eyes narrowed. "You're hoping he bugged it, aren't you?"

"I want to give Brancotti every opportunity to assure himself that we are who we say we are. Most of the others he invited for his little auction are returning clients. Steven Bradford is an unknown, and Brancotti is very cautious."

Natalie had to hand it to him for thinking of allowing Brancotti to wire the plane. Everything so far about the cover that Chance had built for them had won her admiration. As far as she could tell, nothing had been overlooked. The small purse she carried contained a driver's license, passport and several well-worn credit cards that identified her as Catherine Weston. The driver's license was from San Diego, California, and would expire in eight months. But if Brancotti ran a check on Catherine Weston, now "Calli," he would find that she'd been born and raised in a small town, nestled in the foothills of the Blue Ridge Mountains.

Under Chance's careful supervision, she'd spent three hours boning up on Catherine Weston's background instead of sleeping. And once the real Calli had arrived at the hotel, Natalie had spent another three hours studying and talking with her.

Natalie stifled a yawn. She hadn't slept more than two hours, but how could she complain when Chance was being just as thorough as she always was when she adopted a new persona. A perfectionist. That was the one word she would use to sum up Chance's approach to this job, and she had no choice but to admire him for it.

She glanced at him and saw that he was using a pocket flashlight to read the open file on his lap. The Steven Bradford disguise was excellent, and as Natalie studied him, she marveled again at how far it went beyond the wrinkled tan suit he was wearing.

The tiny lines that furrowed his brow as he frowned at something he was reading were new. So was the way he ran his fingers absently through his hair. Body language, she knew, was as important as the costume in creating an authentic disguise. She watched his fingers toy with the edges of the manila folder on his lap, folding the edge back and forth. She would have been willing to bet that Chance Mitchell had never fidgeted in his life. He was the most self-contained man she'd ever met. The only time she was certain of what was on his mind was when they were making love.

What would the man sitting across from her be like in bed? Would the perfectionist streak in Chance force him to carry the impersonation of Steven Bradford that far?

One thing Natalie did know from the time she'd spent with the real Catherine Weston—the woman's relationship with Steven Bradford went beyond her ambition to become a supermodel. The dreamy look in her eyes when she'd spoken about Steven was a dead giveaway. Natalie would have bet good money that Catherine Weston had fallen hard for the software billionaire.

Did Chance's Steven Bradford have similar feelings for his Calli, she wondered? If so, she had no doubt that Chance would have carefully noted it in that mental notebook she suspected he carried with him. What would the perfectionist in him force him to do with the knowledge?

One thing Natalie knew for certain—her Calli was not going to wait much longer to find out. One of the many things she'd learned about her namesake was that she had boundless energy and enthusiasm—and Natalie was sure it extended to the physical side of her relationship with Steven Bradford. Gut instinct told her that Catherine Weston had even fewer hang-ups than Rachel Cade. And she couldn't wait to try out that facet of Calli's personality.

A sliver of pure excitement shot up her spine. For the first time, she admitted to herself how much she really wanted to work at Chance's side during this operation. She was definitely her father's daughter, and for the first time in her life, she wasn't going to feel guilty about embracing that part of herself. Instead, she was going to enjoy it, and she was also going to enjoy exploring a relationship with Chance.

There'd be a price to pay. There always was. But as she watched Chance turn his flashlight off and insert it in the breast pocket of his shirt, she knew that however she was going to pay for saying yes to Chance Mitchell's proposition, she was sure it was going to be worth it.

And she had plans for him. He'd evidently been satisfied after one night with Natalie. And last night he'd been able to resist making love to Rachel. But his one-night stand days were over. Calli was going to see to that.

CHANCE WAS very much aware of Natalie's eyes on him. Just as he was fully aware of the excitement radiating from her in little spurts. She might look like Calli, but right now her body language was totally Natalie's. Her arms were folded across her chest and her foot was tapping. He knew exactly what she was feeling because he felt it, too. He was equally impatient for the adventure to begin. There was nothing like going up against a worthy and challenging opponent.

What worried him a little was that challenging Brancotti wasn't all that was on his mind. He was also thinking of being with Natalie. And those thoughts were distracting him from the file he was reading. It was taking him twice as long as usual to memorize Tracker's latest surveillance map of the Brancotti estate. Swamps bordered the estate on two sides, and they were kept well stocked with alligators. That left two avenues for escape in an emergency. Through the entrance gate on the western side or by boat on the ocean side.

A red dot just inside the southern edge of the swamp marked where Tracker had hidden an inflatable boat. Hopefully, all would go well, and they could use it to meet Tracker once they had the Ferrante diamond.

Pocketing the flashlight, Chance closed the file and for the first time since they'd entered the limo, he met Natalie's eyes. "Ready?"

"What did you have in mind?"

The grin she flashed him and the quick arch of her back told Chance he was dealing with Calli now. As Rachel, Natalie was slower moving and much more aware of her effect on the opposite sex. She knew to a *T* what she had in her arsenal, and she matched the weapon to the man.

Calli was more spontaneous, and her heart ruled her head. She didn't even think about attracting men, but everything she did, including the back stretch, was incredibly sexy.

"You're very good at impersonation," he said. So good that he was wondering how being Calli would affect her response the next time he touched her.

"So are you." She pushed her hair behind her ear.

"Right now I'm wondering what it will be like to make love to Steven Bradford."

"Rachel, I—"

She leaned closer, and he caught her scent.

"Aren't you wondering what it will be like to make love to Calli? We could find out." She reached for his tie, but before she could pull it off, he grabbed her hands.

"We're almost to the airport. If you've got any questions about the plan once we get to the estate, now would be a good time to ask them."

Natalie raised her brows. "Plan? I wouldn't call what we have a plan exactly."

"Sure it is," Chance said easily. "Find the safe, pick a time to crack it, replace the real diamond with the fake one that Brancotti left behind the last time, and then leave."

"It's a little short on the details," Natalie pointed out.

Chance was beginning to enjoy himself. Whether she realized it or not, Detective Natalie Gibbs was beginning to shine through, and he found he'd missed her. "You'll just have to trust me. We'll improvise the details as we go. If you're nervous, you can just follow my lead." He regarded her steadily for a moment. "Unless you think you can't keep up."

Her chin lifted, and Chance had to bite back a grin.

"I'm way ahead of you," she said. "My plan is to charm Carlo into giving me a tour of the house and see if I can spot the safe."

Chance frowned. "It'll be better if we take the tour together."

As the limousine pulled to a stop, she shot him a Calli smile. "Relax. I'm pretty sure my plan will work faster."

"You can't be too obvious."

Her brows shot up. "I can be very subtle when I want to."

Natalie didn't worry him. It was Calli who made him nervous.

Before she got out of the car, she patted him on the knee. "You'll just have to follow *my* lead."

NATALIE GIBBS slept like a rock, Chance thought as he sat across from her, watching her. She'd curled up on the seat across from his the moment the aircraft had reached cruising altitude. When they'd hit some turbulence over Virginia, she hadn't stirred, not even when he'd pressed his hands briefly against her to keep her on the couch.

He'd been tempted to do more than touch her, but he'd resisted—just as he'd resisted making love to her last night. It had been late when she'd finished her session with Catherine Weston, and he'd pretended to be asleep when she'd slipped into bed beside him. Oh, he'd been tempted then to turn and see which of the two women had joined him—Rachel or Calli. But he'd resisted. And he would be wise to continue resisting until the job was done.

Of course, that was much easier said than done. She was stretched full length on the seat across from his, and she was wearing "Calli" clothes—a stretchy, midriff-baring tank top and shorts. Looking at her was not helping to strengthen his resolve. Taking a quick sip of the ice water he'd poured for himself, he decided to take a break from his self-imposed torture and browse through his file on Brancotti once more.

NATALIE CAME AWAKE in stages the way she always did, and out of habit she remained perfectly still until all the layers of fog in her brain had disappeared. The hum of the jet's engine told her where she was, and she could feel Chance's presence as well as smell him. Was he looking at her? She'd selected her outfit with the main purpose of making him do just that. And she'd posed herself on the couch to tempt him while she slept.

That was step one of her plan. Now it was time for step two.

Keeping her eyes closed, she stretched and felt the tank top inch its way upward. Then in one smooth movement, she sat up and opened her eyes.

Humph. He wasn't looking at her. Instead, he was sitting, shoulders hunched, poring over his file. And he had horn-rimmed reading glasses perched on the bridge of his nose. For some reason, just looking at him wearing them had a little tendril of lust uncurling itself in her stomach.

Oh, it was more than time for step three.

"Steven?" she said in her high, effervescent Calli voice.

"Hmmmm?" Chance didn't even glance up from the papers he was reading.

It was damned hard to seduce a man when he wouldn't even look at her. Good thing she had a fool-proof plan.

Taking the file out of his hands, she slid onto his lap. "Hi."

"Calli—"

"Shhhh." She cut him off by pressing a finger against his lips. "I've been wanting to do this ever since I came back to the hotel last night."

He closed his fingers around her wrist and drew her hand away. "We'll be landing in a very short—"

This time she cut him off by pressing her lips against his. The heat ignited immediately, leaping from her to him and back again. Drawing away, she said, "I can be very quick." As if to prove it, she slid to her knees and pulled his belt free, unbuttoned his trousers and slid the zipper down.

When his hand covered hers again, she drew back a little and tugged her tank over her head. "I want you, Steven." She touched him then, taking him into her hand. "You want me, too. You always want me, don't you, Steven?"

HE DID. Later, Chance told himself that if he'd had a moment to think before she'd taken him into her hands… If she hadn't called him "Steven," or looked at him in that particular way… Or maybe if he hadn't been looking at her for the past hour and fantasizing about taking her on the floor of the airplane… Maybe then he would have been able to resist her and stick to his resolution.

He couldn't think at all when she rose to her feet and wiggled out of her shorts.

She was wearing nothing underneath. His hands came to life then, pulling her so that she could straddle him. And then she was taking him into her. Only then did she lift his glasses off and set them on the table.

"We wouldn't want to fog these up, would we?" she asked before she found his mouth again and began to move.

9

THE LATE-AFTERNOON SUN beat down mercilessly as the limousine turned onto a sleekly paved drive. The limo had been waiting for them when the plane touched down on Brancotti's private landing field. The driver, a tall blond muscle builder in his mid-twenties, had assured them that the twenty-minute ride would be as cool and as comfortable as he could make it. In her persona as Calli, Natalie didn't have to hide the fact that she was totally impressed with the chilled champagne and the fruit and cheese tray that awaited them in the plush interior of the limousine. Mozart poured out of a speaker, and she sat cross-legged on the carpeted floor, turning the knobs on a small TV.

Unless and until they could be absolutely certain that they weren't being bugged, they were to stay completely in character. That was the plan, and Natalie decided that being Calli was liberating. The woman didn't seem to have any hang-ups.

And seducing Steven Bradford had been almost as exciting as seducing Chance Mitchell. There'd been an added kick to realize that initially he'd tried to resist her. It occurred to her that she'd never before tried to seduce a reluctant man. But once Steven had gotten over his initial resistance, he'd been a more than willing participant. And if she hadn't known better, she would have sworn that the man she'd made love with on the airplane was different than the one she'd made love to two nights ago. As a lover Steven was gentler, or perhaps sweeter was a better word.

Did Chance feel the same way about Calli—that she was a different lover from Rachel? Which woman did he prefer? The thought fascinated her. Gazing over her shoulder, she studied him for a minute. It was definitely Steven she was looking at. What would it be like if she could make him lose control and become Chance when he wanted to be Steven Bradford?

Running her hand along the lush carpeting, she considered what it might be like to discover the answer to her question right now. Right here.

Turning, she sent Chance a slow smile. "Want to fool around?"

Without taking his eyes off of the papers he was poring over, he threaded his fingers absently through her hair. "Later. I have a call with Harold scheduled for five o'clock, and I need to get through these."

The call would be with Tracker McBride. That much Natalie knew. The conversation would sound like business, but there would be a coded subtext. Right now the subtext of his message to her was to keep her mind on the job.

But wasn't part of her job establishing the fact that she was totally besotted with Steven Bradford? Knowing that the driver was listening and probably watching through his rearview mirror, Natalie twisted around and placed her hand on Chance's thigh. "You know what they say about all work and no play."

In a quick move that she didn't anticipate, Chance closed his hands over her shoulders and drew her close for a long, hard kiss. Then even as heat flared to life, he moved his mouth to her ear and whispered, "You're playing with fire."

She laughed. "I hope so."

She felt his lips curve as he brushed soft kisses at the corners of her mouth. There it was again, that unexpected gentleness. Was it part of Chance or merely a layer to the persona of Steven Bradford? She was leaning forward when he slipped his hands out of her hair and set her away from him.

"Too late. We're here," he murmured.

Glancing through the window, she saw that they'd stopped at a mammoth gate set in a tall stone fence. The moment it opened, the limo slid through and continued up a winding narrow drive. Flowers bloomed on either side. To the right, there were three tennis courts where two hardy souls battled the heat and each other. Through the tall cypresses to her left she caught a glimpse of a landscaped patio area surrounding a huge pool. A few guests sat sipping drinks in the shade of red-and-white striped umbrellas.

Then as the car swept around a curve and the main house came into view, Natalie let her mouth drop open. The building was huge, three stories high with wings on either side. The entire structure was built out of slabs of gray marble streaked with shades of rose and pink. It reminded her of an Italian villa as she supposed it was meant to. At its right stood a low-slung building—an old carriage house, she guessed. Now it probably served as a garage and servants' quarters.

"Wow," she said as the car pulled to a stop. Though she didn't repeat it, she might have said the same about the man who descended the marble steps to greet them. In person, Carlo Brancotti was even better-looking than he'd been in the photos Chance had shown her.

Tall and broad-shouldered, he wore black trousers and a white shirt with the sleeves rolled up. But it was his face that drew and held her attention as Chance guided her out of the limo. The slash of cheekbones and the hair hanging loose to his shoulders made her think of ancient warriors. The hint of the savage in contrast with the elegant clothes and surroundings made for a devastating effect. She had a moment to absorb the impression as he shook hands with Steven Bradford. When he took her hand and looked into her eyes, a quick prickle of unease moved through her.

For a second, just until he released her hand, she had the uncanny sensation that he could see right through her. It passed the moment he smiled at her.

"I'm so glad I made an exception and allowed Steven to bring you along."

"So am I." The smile she sent him was genuine. "You have a lovely place."

"It's even lovelier now," he said. Lifting a hand, he signaled for a man who wore a uniform identical to the one the driver had worn. "Show Mr. Bradford and Miss Calli to the Venetian room." Then he turned to Steven. "Make yourselves at home in any way you wish. I'm giving a small party tonight so that my guests can get to know one another."

Steven frowned. "I'm a busy man. I didn't come to party."

Brancotti smiled and shook his head. "So American. You'll have to learn to relax and enjoy my hospitality."

Then he turned and led the way into the house.

A PRICKLE OF UNEASE had worked its way up Chance's spine the moment that Carlo had said the words *Venetian room*. It moved through him once more as he read the same words on the engraved brass plate that adorned the door to the suite they were shown into. Venetia and *Venetian*. Was the name of the suite a coincidence or Carlo's way of letting him know that he was aware of who he was?

A part of his mind said no. There was no one at the agency who knew that he was coming here as Steven Bradford. Still, his mind raced as he watched Natalie move around the suite and peer through the French doors that led to a small balcony. She was playing her part beautifully, just the right mixture of sex kitten and wide-eyed innocent. And he was finding the combination fascinating. So damn fascinating that in spite of his resolution, he hadn't been able to resist her when she'd begun to seduce him on the plane.

"Look, we have a view of the pool and the ocean." Then she was skirting around the valet who'd escorted them to the room, and opening the door to an adjoining bath.

"Wow!" she said. "The shower takes up the whole wall, and there's a hot tub."

"Will there be anything else, sir?" the valet asked.

"No." Chance followed the valet to the door. Before he closed it, he glanced once more at the brass plate.

Brancotti might suspect any one of the guests he'd invited to the estate. He might even put Steven Bradford at the top of his list. But he couldn't know for sure.

Still, he should tell Natalie that they might be under suspicion. When he turned back into the room, she was moving through the suite, running her hands over the polished surfaces of old antiques, oohing and aahing. If Brancotti was listening, he'd hear a girl raised in the foothills of the Blue Ridge Mountains nearly going into ecstasy over his home. He might be rattled, but Detective Natalie Gibbs was doing her job, checking for any hidden cameras or small microphones.

Emotions streamed through him—admiration and something he couldn't quite put a name to. She was getting to him, and for both their sakes, he couldn't let that distract him from the job he'd come here to do.

"This is so lovely," she cooed as she climbed onto the bed and ran her fingers over the carved headboard. Then she stretched out on the mattress and sent him a quick grin. "Any idea about what we could do to while the time away until that dinner party?"

"You could take a swim in the pool," he suggested.

"Too hot." She made a face as she rolled over and then dropped her chin on her hands.

"I need to work," he said.

She made another face. "Too boring."

Moving to the bed, he took her hand and drew her up and off the mattress. "Why don't you try out the hot tub?"

She locked her arms around his neck. "Why don't we try it out together?"

"I really need to get some work done." But he leaned closer, caught the lobe of her ear between his teeth and whispered, "What did you find?"

Keeping her arms looped around his neck, she drew back and mouthed the words. "No cameras, two mikes here in the bedroom. One mike in the bathroom." Then she said aloud, "Oh, Steven, you worked on the plane."

"I need to talk to you," he whispered right against her ear. "Tonight, during the party, find an excuse to entice me away for a while. We'll walk along the beach."

"Oh, Steven." Her voice was a throaty purr as she drew back again. "You're always working. Can't we play? Just a little?"

Pursing her lips in a little pout, she pulled his tie loose. Then before he could even think to stop her, she was working on his belt.

"Calli."

"I want you."

Quite suddenly, he wanted her. Calli, Rachel, Natalie. They were all parts of the same woman, and he wanted them all. But they had a job. They should both rest.

The thought slipped away as her hand enclosed him.

"You know I can't go for very long without sex. It's a curse." She kissed him then, making sure that every soft curve of her body was pressed fully against his.

Chance flipped on the stereo beside the bed to mask the noises he knew they would make and then eased her back onto the mattress. "Then we're both damned."

NATALIE HAD to hand it to Carlo Brancotti. The man knew how to throw a party. Dinner had been a sumptuous seven-course affair served in a room that reminded her of a medieval dining hall. Her dinner partner had been a portly British gentleman, Sir Arthur Latham, who'd seemed sincerely interested in Calli's aspirations in the modeling field. The woman on her left had looked vaguely familiar, but it wasn't until Sir Arthur had introduced her that Natalie realized she was Risa Manwaring, a retired actress who had married a British lord.

By the time they'd finished with dessert, Risa had the name of her agent as well as a list of her most recent modeling jobs.

At the far end of the table, "Steven" had been seated to Carlo's immediate right, and as far as she could tell, the conversation between the two men hadn't flagged once.

Were she and Chance being tested—or was she just being paranoid? Natalie had always found that when she was doing undercover work, a little paranoia was a good thing. But hers had been increasing steadily from the moment she'd looked into Carlo Brancotti's eyes that afternoon.

She was pretty sure that Chance was feeling the same way. She'd felt the tension in him escalate the moment they'd entered their suite. There'd been that urgent request that she lure him away from the party. And she'd sensed an even greater urgency when they'd made love. What did he need to tell her?

Whatever it was, he was willing to wait until they

could be absolutely sure that no one was eavesdropping. So it was important, but not urgent.

The gathering at dinner had been small—under a dozen in all. Besides Sir Arthur and Lady Latham and the retired film star, there'd been two Japanese gentlemen, the Motos—father and son. Natalie recognized them as the two men she'd seen playing tennis earlier in the day. She'd also been introduced to the Demirs, a distinguished-looking businessman and his wife from Turkey, and another man with very hard eyes— Armand Genovese. Carlo's personal assistant Lisa had rounded out the number. Though she wasn't sure why, Natalie had expected more guests.

Once Carlo had led the way from the dining room to the conservatory for after-dinner drinks, the men had retired to the patio to sample some of his cigars. Natalie had toyed with the idea of joining them and insisting on sampling one herself, but had decided at the last moment that it wasn't something that Calli would have done.

Instead, she joined the four other women as Lisa led them on a guided tour of the flowers growing in the conservatory. It wasn't difficult to keep her expression awestruck as she admired more varieties of orchids than she'd ever seen. The fact was, she wasn't finding it difficult at all to be Catherine Weston.

Maybe it was the fact that the woman was about as uncomplicated as they came. She'd come from nothing and her ticket to the big time in modeling was Steven Bradford. Natalie Gibbs might not have gone about it the same way, but she could certainly admire Calli's single-minded determination to make a different kind of life for herself.

After all, wasn't that what she'd tried to do with her own life? For twenty-six years she'd lived with the fear that she was her father's daughter—that she might be tempted to follow in his footsteps. She'd joined the D.C. police because she'd wanted to make sure that she satisfied her desire for adventure on the right side of the law.

And now as Calli she had the opportunity to have her cake and eat it, too. A diamond heist—it didn't get much better than that.

She was even beginning to like the wardrobe that Chance had picked out for Calli. Natalie fingered the spaghetti straps that held up the silky white sheath she was wearing. Whether or not they made the man, clothes definitely made the woman. Each time she dressed in one of the outfits, she felt that she came to a deeper understanding of the part she was playing. Or perhaps, she was coming to a deeper understanding of herself.

When she'd slipped into the silky white dress that Chance had selected for her tonight, she'd instantly felt both beautiful and desirable. Natalie Gibbs rarely allowed herself to feel either of those ways.

But then the old Natalie would never have worn a dress that stopped at midthigh. Nor would she have thought of seducing a man twice in one day. No, three times. She had plans for that walk on the beach.

"It's a lovely room, isn't it?"

Natalie turned to smile at Sir Arthur's wife, Lady Latham. "I've never seen anything quite like it."

The glass walls and ceiling of the conservatory allowed a view of a starlit sky, and the air was scented with exotic flowers and candle wax. A small band tucked in a corner and surrounded by potted palms was playing a movie theme she couldn't quite place.

"But you're missing your young man?"

Natalie smiled. "A bit."

"Carlo is European and old-fashioned. He still honors an old tradition that men and women separate for a time after dinner. That is not the case in America, am I correct?"

"Yes, that is not the case in America."

Lady Latham smiled at her. "Well, maybe you were right to fight for your independence. But don't tell Sir Arthur I said that."

Natalie pantomimed locking her lips and then throwing away the key. She was beginning to like Lady Latham very much.

"You ought to go out there and lure your Steven away. A man with someone like you doesn't need imported cigars or the poker game that Carlo will entice them into next."

Natalie studied the woman for a minute. Though she was well into her sixties, she could see that Lady Latham must have been quite a beauty in her day. The smile she saw in the pale gray eyes looked sincere. "I promised Steven to be on my best behavior tonight. He wants to conclude his business with Carlo as quickly as possible."

Lady Latham's brows shot up. "There won't be any business done until tomorrow or the next day. Hassam Aldiri's plane was delayed, and he won't arrive until tomorrow afternoon at the earliest. Carlo will wait for him. Hassam has a lot of money. Even if he decides that he doesn't want the diamond, I doubt that Carlo will want to offend him."

"Well…in that case." Flashing Lady Latham a conspiratorial smile, she moved toward the doors she'd seen the men exit through earlier. The night air was warm in spite of the breeze from the ocean, but one quick glance told her that the patio was empty. Hurrying toward the balustrade that separated it from the sprawl of gardens below, she caught sight of the men seated at tables in a small candlelit gazebo.

"I understand Steven has a weakness for poker."

Natalie pressed a hand to her heart as she turned to face Carlo. She hadn't heard him approach. "Yes, he can never resist a game. How did you know?"

"I make it a point to get to know the people I do business with."

Though she couldn't see his eyes as clearly as she had earlier, Natalie felt the intensity of his gaze. "I was hoping to lure him away for a walk on the beach."

Carlo held out his arm. "Perhaps you'll allow me to stand in for him?"

"No, I don't think so," Natalie said with a shy smile. "I had more than walking in mind."

"Ah." Lifting a hand, he drew a finger down her cheek. "I would be delighted to be his substitute for that also."

"Oh no. I could *never*…" She and Chance had discussed the possibility that Carlo would make a move on her, but she hadn't expected it to be so soon.

For a moment he said nothing. Natalie waited. She was pretty sure that Carlo Brancotti was not a man who accepted rejection easily. This might blow her chance of ever getting that private tour. Finally, she saw the quick flash of his smile. "I admire loyalty. It's a precious commodity."

Natalie eased away a step so that he was forced to withdraw his hand. The last thing she wanted to do was alienate Carlo Brancotti, but she had no choice except to react to the situation the way she believed that Catherine Weston would react. "I don't want to interrupt Steven's game, so I think I'll retire to my room," she said.

"I apologize if I offended you. I want you to feel perfectly comfortable and enjoy your stay here." He smiled again and held out his hand. "Could we, as you Americans say, wipe the slate clean and begin again?"

"Sure." She put her hand in his and felt the warm press of his palm before he released hers.

When she turned to go back into the conservatory, he placed a hand on her arm. "Please. I will feel that I have failed as a host if you retire so early. How about if I offer you a tour of the gardens or the house—or both?"

Natalie hesitated, then smiled. "I'd love to see both. Steven has a couple of great homes—a ranch and a house he just built outside of L.A.—but I've never seen anything like this place. How old is it?"

"It's relatively new." He didn't touch her but merely held his hand out to indicate the direction. "I bought the house from a Saudi Prince two years ago, but the gardens are new. Flowers are my passion."

"I admire anyone who can grow things," she said enthusiastically as he guided her down a circular stair. "Not that I have a green thumb. I don't. But I love flowers."

"It's a passion that we share then," Carlo said as he urged her toward a door beneath the stairs. "Shall we start with the house and save the best until last?"

10

CHANCE HELD three royal ladies in his hand, but the woman who held his attention wasn't in the cards he'd been dealt. She was standing on the patio talking to Carlo Brancotti. And she could handle herself. Wasn't that the reason he'd been so determined to get Natalie Gibbs for this job?

"Are you in, Mr. Bradford?"

Silently cursing himself, Chance glanced back down at his cards.

Natalie was focused on the job. He was the one who was allowing himself to be distracted. The truth was that whenever he made love to her he became so drawn into the moment that he almost forgot that he was here to do a job. When he glanced back up at the patio, it was empty.

Chance ruthlessly suppressed the mix of panic and anger that tangled in his stomach. Natalie had made her plan clear. She was going to persuade Carlo to give her a tour. Obviously, the plan was working.

But Venetia had been following a plan, too.

"Are you in or out?" Armand Genovese's voice was thin with impatience.

"Give me a minute." Chance tore his gaze away

from the patio and found four pairs of eyes staring at him. What he read in them ran the gamut from annoyance and mild curiosity to speculation and amusement. It was the speculation that bothered him the most because it came from Sir Arthur Latham, the man he suspected would report his every move to Carlo.

Get a grip, he warned himself. He could hardly throw down his cards and go running after Natalie. One of Steven Bradford's weaknesses was poker. He had a group of friends, ones who went back to the founding of his company, that he regularly played with. Chance had to believe that Brancotti's dossier on Bradford would have included that little known piece of information. So he could only conclude that the poker game had been arranged to keep "Steven" occupied and separated from "Calli" for the evening.

"Mr. Bradford?" The question came from the Turkish man who was also clearly annoyed.

"I think that Mr. Bradford may be thinking of other ways that he could be spending the evening," Sir Arthur said. "And I can't say that I blame him."

Chance pushed a pile of chips into the center. "I'm in."

For the rest of the hand, he kept his attention focused on the game. Natalie was doing her job. If he wanted to keep her safe, all he had to do was concentrate on doing his.

"YOU DID SAVE the best for last," Natalie said as Carlo led the way down a winding path bordered on either side by jewel-colored flowers.

"You delight me. Most women are more impressed with the main salon or the gallery," Carlo said.

"They were lovely, too. But the paintings in the gallery made it seem more like a…museum." She sent him an apologetic smile. "I'm not much on museums."

As they continued down the path, Natalie reviewed the tour Carlo had just given her in her mind. He'd taken her through all of the rooms on the first floor—except for one that had a coded access pad. His workspace, he'd said as he'd guided her past it. Then for the length of a long hallway, he hadn't spoken. Natalie suspected that he was waiting for her to ask to see it. She hadn't. Instead, she'd stopped to "ooh" and "aah" over a marble-topped table with a mosaic inlay.

Gut instinct told her she was still being tested. Did he suspect that she wasn't the real Calli or was he always this careful?

The main salon took up the entire first floor in the wing opposite the conservatory. Marble floors gleamed, mirrored walls caught the reflections of carved pillars and crystal chandeliers. French doors opened onto patios with a view of the ocean. Natalie had spotted at least two surveillance cameras.

"The masquerade ball will be held in here tomorrow night," Carlo had said. "Who will you come as?"

Natalie had realized that she didn't know so she'd shot him a flustered look. "I can't tell you that. Steven says the whole point of a masquerade is that no one knows who you are. For one night you get to be someone else entirely with no consequences."

"How will I find you?" Carlo had asked. "All I would ask for is a dance."

Hoping for the best, Natalie had allowed herself to remain a bit flustered. "I really can't tell you. Steven hasn't even told *me* what costumes he brought."

Carlo had laughed. "You're charming. Steven is a very lucky man. But I will still try to figure out who you are."

Which wouldn't be much of a challenge, Natalie had thought. She'd spotted two cameras in the hallways, and Carlo would see them leaving the Venetian room in whatever they were wearing.

"I do love playing games. I believe your Steven does too," Carlo had said as he'd taken her arm and drawn her back to the main hall. "Come, I want to show you something."

The something had been a small room down the hallway. Oval in shape, it boasted two ornately carved pillars at the midpoint of the room.

"This gallery is my favorite place. We'll have the auction here. What do you think?"

"Wow," she'd said as she'd let her gaze sweep the room. Furniture was positioned to form conversation areas on richly hued oriental rugs, and settees were placed at intervals along one wall. Across from them hung the paintings.

Natalie had counted ten, and she'd been hard pressed to keep her mouth from falling open. She'd recognized several of the painters, but she hadn't been sure that Calli would.

"It's like you have your own museum," she said. And while Calli had stared in awestruck wonder, Natalie had catalogued the pieces in her mind. There were two van Goghs, a Manet and what she was pretty sure was a Renoir. But there were other works whose artists she wasn't as familiar with. Just how many of them had Carlo Brancotti acquired legitimately?

As if in answer, Carlo had stopped midway down the length of the room, leaned against one of the pillars and told an amusing story of how he'd won one of the van Goghs in a poker game.

Watching him, Natalie had felt a kind of prickling at the back of her neck, one that she hadn't felt in a very long time. She hadn't dared look around to figure out what had caused it because she'd had to appear utterly fascinated by Carlo's story. The pillar he'd leaned against was ornately carved and right behind his head was what looked to be a bronze sundial. The prickling sensation had increased.

The moment Carlo had finished his story, she'd smiled. "If you're that good at poker, you should be out with Steven and your other guests."

"Then I would have missed this opportunity to share my most prized possessions with you," Carlo had replied as he'd led her back outside.

His most prized possessions. Now, as they toured the gardens, the phrase lingered in her mind. And what was in that room that had made the back of her neck prickle like that?

"The gardens are boring you," Carlo said.

With a start, Natalie jerked her thoughts firmly back to the present. "No, they're magical. Sorry." She made the first excuse she could think of. "I guess I'm just missing Steven."

"You're in love with him, aren't you?" Carlo asked.

"No—I—" To her complete astonishment, Natalie felt herself blush. "We're just…I…he doesn't want…"

Carlo put one finger under her chin, tipping her face up so that he could see it.

Natalie felt a skip of panic as she stared up into those dark eyes. What would he see? For an instant there, she hadn't been sure whether she was speaking as Natalie or as Calli.

She held her breath through a stretch of silence before Carlo dropped his hand and said, "Steven is a very lucky man."

Carlo then gestured her forward, and for a while they walked in silence. The garden path was covered with a soft green mulch and bordered by lights. At regular intervals miniature streetlamps were nestled between palms.

"How clever of you to install the lights," she said finally. "I feel as if I'm walking through a fairyland."

"I had them installed because the temperatures are often so hot here in South Florida, and I wanted my guests to be able to enjoy the gardens once the heat of the day had passed."

The streetlamps also offered the perfect places to install video surveillance equipment. Natalie was certain she'd spotted a tiny camera beneath the ornate shade of the light they'd just passed. She bet there were microphones, too. Carlo Brancotti was a very suspicious and very careful man.

Turning, she shot him a very steady look. "And yet you offer entertainment that keeps your guests otherwise occupied."

He smiled at her. "Sometimes I prefer to enjoy the

gardens under less crowded conditions. Come, there's a new orchid I want to show you over there."

Though she kept her pace slow and her attention focused on the varieties of blooms that Carlo was pointing out to her, Natalie was thinking about the man walking next to her. Not once since he'd told her that he admired loyalty had he tried to touch her in any kind of personal way. Yes, he'd made it clear he wanted to dance with her, but even when he'd tipped her chin up to study her face, his touch had been impersonal. He was being a charming host and very much the gentleman—a persona that was a far right turn from the man she'd read about in the file Chance had compiled.

But there were reasons other than romance why he might want to separate her from Steven. There'd been that moment in the gallery and another when he'd bypassed his "workspace" that she'd felt something. Did he suspect that she and Steven weren't who they pretended to be? She couldn't rid her mind of the certainty that this whole tour was some kind of test.

Natalie the cop would use this opportunity to pump him for information, so she didn't. Instead, she yawned, then glanced guiltily at Carlo. "I'm sorry. It's not the company. Steven woke me very early for the flight here."

"Come. I'll take you inside."

"And Steven?"

"Sometimes the poker games go on into the morning hours."

She allowed disappointment to show in her eyes before she glanced away. "Oh."

"If you wish, I'll send him to you," Carlo offered as he led her back along the path.

She shook her head. "No. He loves the game. It's his one vice."

When they reached the door that he'd escorted her through earlier, he opened it. "If you go in this way, you can avoid the others in the conservatory."

She met his eyes again. "Thank you. Your home is lovely."

Natalie walked down the hallway without a backward glance. And she made very sure not to glance at the door with the coded access pad that led to Carlo's "workspace."

CHANCE FOUND himself glancing at his watch for the fourth time in two hours. Natalie had not reappeared on the patio, and neither had Carlo Brancotti. He'd managed to keep his mind on the game, and he'd even managed to win a few hands. But he hadn't been able to shake off the urge he had to go to Natalie. The rational side of him told him that she was perfectly capable of handling a man like Brancotti.

But each moment that ticked by made him feel less and less reasonable. Chance shoved a pile of chips into the center of the table and waited for the other bets to be placed. When Sir Arthur turned over his full house, Chance laid down his cards and pushed himself away from the table. "I'm finished, gentlemen."

There were a few grumbles. Chance paid them no heed as he let himself out of the screened gazebo and strode back toward the house. He might be making a mistake. He'd been weighing the odds of that for the past two hours. Logic told him that Steven Bradford would stay at the game. But gut instinct told him that he had to go to Natalie, and he hadn't gotten where he was by ignoring his instincts.

Let Carlo Brancotti make what he wanted of the fact that Steven Bradford was so besotted and so hot for Calli that not even a high-stakes poker game could keep him distracted for very long.

The conservatory was empty when he moved through it. At another time, he might have paused to enjoy the orchids, but now he only quickened his stride. There were surveillance cameras everywhere. Not surprising since there were expensive pieces of pottery and sculpture on display even in the hallways. But then, Chance didn't think that anyone Carlo invited to his estate would dare to steal from him.

No. The state-of-the-art surveillance equipment was for keeping tabs on his guests' movements. Chance took the stairs two at a time. If Carlo was watching, he would see a man who was desperate to get to his woman. And Chance was. He needed to see her, to satisfy himself that she was all right.

He needed *her.* Chance felt himself rocked by the realization. Before he had time to absorb or reflect on that, he reached the door to the Venetian room. It was locked. As it should be, he told himself as he swore silently and searched in his pocket for the key.

NATALIE PACED back and forth inside the suite. Since she'd come back to the room, she'd gone over everything that had happened that evening—from the time Carlo had appeared on the balcony to when he'd let her

into the house, making sure she walked by his office
again.

He'd definitely wanted to know about her relationship with Steven Bradford. And she had to hope that
it had rung true. She'd blushed, for heaven's sake. And
she was almost positive that it was Natalie's cheeks
that had heated, not Calli's. When panic threatened to
bubble up again, she ruthlessly pushed it down. She
was not going to worry about that now.

Natalie paused in front of a mirror and faced her reflection. She was playing a game. That was all. Calli
was in love with Steven Bradford. But Natalie was not
falling in love with Chance Mitchell. What she felt for
Chance was lust. And professional respect. The emotions tumbling around inside of her had no relation to
what Catherine Weston felt for Steven Bradford. She
couldn't afford to let the different roles she was playing merge. Giving herself a nod, she began to pace
again.

Gut instinct told her that Carlo Brancotti had not
only been testing her, he'd also been playing some
kind of a game with her. Her mind kept circling back
to the fact that the tour had been his idea. He'd wanted
her to see the layout of the house, his "workspace," the
salon and his gallery. Why?

She stopped pacing and began to tap her foot. It was
in the gallery that her neck had begun to prickle. She
often got that feeling when something meshed for her
on a case. She and Chance had assumed that the Ferrante diamond would be locked in a safe in his office.
Could it be in the gallery?

A quick glance at her watch told her it was midnight, the witching hour. There was no telling when the poker game would break up, and she needed to talk to Chance. Foot still tapping, she considered her options. As Natalie, she'd have to think of a plan. At the very least, Rachel would have to run through the possible repercussions. Thankfully, all Calli had to do was to go down to that poker game and tell Steven that she needed a walk on the beach before she could sleep.

She was at the door when she heard the knob turn, and she opened it just as Chance was fishing out his key. What she saw stopped her short for a moment. His hair was mussed, his expression impatient and just a bit dangerous. Her mouth began to water. But it was what she saw in his eyes—the mix of frustration and desire that had her heart taking a tumble. For just a second, she couldn't move, couldn't even think.

CARLO STUDIED the TV screens in the security room adjacent to his office. One of the security men had buzzed him the moment that Steven Bradford had left the poker game. And now Bradford was standing in the doorway to his room.

"What do you think?" he asked Lisa.

"He's a man who prefers his woman to a poker game," Lisa said.

"But it's well known that poker is his weakness. He plays twice a month with old friends. He doesn't rush home to be with his Calli."

"Perhaps that's because he's playing with friends. Or perhaps he was overcome by jealousy when you spent over an hour giving his Calli a tour of the house and gardens."

Carlo glanced at her sharply. Something in her tone told him that she didn't approve, but it wasn't like her to criticize him. "Are you jealous, too?"

She met his eyes, but said nothing.

"You don't think the tour was wise."

"No. You haven't yet decided who the plant is, and yet you showed her the gallery where the safe is."

Carlo smiled then and lifted a hand to trace it along her cheek. "Where one of my safes is."

"You're playing with fire."

"It's just a bit of misdirection, my dear Lisa. And I know what I'm doing. If they think the Ferrante diamond is in the gallery safe, it will make the game more interesting. And you can stop being jealous. My other guests will receive the same tour."

"I still don't like it," Lisa said.

He leaned down and brushed his mouth over hers. When her lips warmed and softened beneath his, he drew back and raised her hand to his lips. "Come. I think we can leave the lovebirds to themselves. And perhaps I can make it up to you for spending so much time with Calli."

FOR JUST A SECOND after Natalie opened the door, Chance couldn't move. Feelings swamped him. She was here. She was safe.

And he didn't have any idea which woman he was looking at. That realization fueled both his frustration and his desire. Stepping forward, he urged her back into the room, closed the door and locked it. Then he grabbed her arms, drew her up on her toes and closed his mouth over hers. Heat. He could feel it shoot from her to him and back again. He wanted, no, he needed…

Drawing back for a moment, he stared at her in the moonlight streaming into the room. *Who are you?* he wanted to ask. He wanted to shout it. But he couldn't.

What he said was, "I want you." Then before she could answer, he pushed her back against the wall and kissed her again. By damn, he was going to find out which part she was playing. He had to.

The flavor would give her away. Rachel was slightly tart. He tasted that. Calli was sweet—like wild honey—and he found that, too. He nipped her bottom lip and discovered the dark exotic flavor that had haunted him for three months. Natalie. Even as all three tastes flooded through him, he was desperate for more. Changing the angle of his head, he took the kiss deeper.

When he dragged himself back this time, they were both panting. In another moment, he would have pulled her to the floor and taken her right there. Scooping her up in his arms, he carried her into the bathroom and kicked the door shut behind him.

He didn't set her down until he'd twisted the knobs of the shower. There was a small mike on the ledge of the hot tub. He wanted to make sure that the spray would block any sound. He said nothing as he began to strip out of his clothes.

Natalie waited, watching as he removed his shirt and allowed his trousers to pool at his feet. In the moonlight pouring through the balcony doors, he looked like a god. She moved closer. Then, placing her hands on his shoulders, she drew his head down and spoke into his ear. "There are cameras throughout the garden, probably microphones, too. And I've been everywhere on the first floor. I know where Carlo's office is."

He gripped her hips and set her far enough away that he could see her eyes. They were a bit puzzled, but focused on his. Did she believe that he'd brought her in here to hear a report? She was thinking of the job and all he was thinking of, all he *could* think of, was her.

"Do you care if that dress gets wet?"

He couldn't hear his own words over the noise of the shower, but she must have read his lips because she turned and pointed to the zipper.

It extended all of three inches down from the small of her back, and as the silk parted, his fingers brushed against soft, damp skin. She shrugged her shoulders, wiggled her hips, and the dress slid to her feet.

She was wearing nothing beneath it. Chance's mouth went dry as a bone. He'd wondered, of course. So had every other man at dinner. But he hadn't known and hadn't truly believed that the woman he'd known originally as Natalie Gibbs would have gone to a dinner party, wearing nothing at all under her dress. Even Rachel Cade had worn underwear, hadn't she? To think she'd spent one hour alone with Carlo Brancotti wearing nothing but that thin swatch of silk.

Turning, Natalie looped her arms around his neck and pulled his ear to her mouth. What was she going to tell him now? That she knew where Brancotti's safe was?

He gripped her shoulders hard. "You can give me the damned report later. First, I want to know who the hell you are."

She didn't answer him immediately, but he could see the way her eyes darkened, the way the pulse at her throat fluttered. Then she smiled and suddenly her mouth was at his ear again. "I can be anyone you want."

Not quite gently, he clamped one arm around her waist and kept the other gripping her arm as he pulled her into the shower with him.

"I can be Rachel." She nipped his earlobe. Somehow she'd managed to get hold of the soap, and her hands slid over his skin leaving trails of ice and fire in their wake.

"I love touching your body." Her voice had become a breathy whisper. "Do you like it when I touch you here?" Her hand slithered from his shoulders down his chest.

"How about here?" Her fingers drew a line to his waist and then lower. "Or here? Do you like this?"

He closed his eyes as her slick, hot fist enclosed him.

"Or I can be Calli." She dropped a quick line of kisses along his jaw and began to pump him gently.

"Or I can be both." Her laugh was a breath in his ear before her tongue darted inside. And then she was whispering, "I could be two women at once. Is that your fantasy, Steven?"

He felt his head literally spin, his strength drain away.

"I could give you your fantasy," she breathed. "Right now, I'm Rachel."

Chance felt the subtle change in her posture. Her hand grew firmer on him and began to move more quickly.

"All during dinner, I thought of doing this. And this." She ran a slick hand over his shoulder and down his back to spread her fingers over his buttocks. "If you'd been sitting next to me, I would have found a way to touch you—even with Lady Latham watching us from across the table. Can you imagine it?"

Her whispered words had the image filling his mind.

"We might have been caught while I was slipping down your zipper, inch by inch. And then I would have done this." Her hand stilled, then milked him in one long pull.

With a moan, Chance slammed one hand against the shower wall to steady himself.

"You like that. Would you like me to make you come this way?"

This was madness. As he lifted his head and tried to clear it, she was all he could see—those wide eyes, the color now as dark and mysterious as the sea at night. That soft, soft mouth. In the misty steam that swirled around them, she made him think of a mermaid, and for the first time in his life, he understood how mythical sirens had lured sailors to their deaths. Those men simply hadn't cared about anything else.

Then she smiled, and releasing him, she stepped closer until the length of his hardness was pressed against her softness. Her mouth was at his ear again.

"Now, I'll be Calli. I'm not nearly as experienced as Rachel, but I read. When I was on the patio watching you play poker, I thought about this wickedly sexy book I read. It was all about what went on in this Victorian brothel. On Friday night, the men would gather in the parlor for a game of cards, and the lady of their choice would crawl under the table, and slip between the gentleman's knees…can you picture that?"

As the image formed in his mind, she slithered down his body and took him into her mouth. He couldn't think, couldn't breathe. He was drowning in her. Everything he was became centered on the sensations she brought him—the movement of that soft, hot mouth, the sharp press of her fingernails as she kneaded them into his backside.

He'd never felt a pleasure so intense. He wanted it to go on forever. But he wanted to be inside of her when he came. The struggle between those two desires was brief and vicious. But he finally found the strength to free himself. He knelt with her on the floor of the shower.

Water sluiced over them. Her wet hair clung to her forehead in jagged wisps, making her look different once again. The thought had barely entered his head, when she drew his ear to her mouth again.

"I'm a stranger you've just met. You don't even know my name." Her quick, wicked laugh only punched up the heat that was boiling inside of him.

"We have no history, no future, no expectations. You just know that you want me. You do want me, don't you, Chance?"

Later he would wonder if it was her use of that name that pushed him to the edge. He didn't know exactly who she was. When he looked into her eyes, all he saw was himself, trapped. All he was certain of was that he needed her with a desperation that threatened to slice him in two.

She smiled, but it wasn't Rachel's smile this time. Nor was it Calli's. "I want you. Now."

Chance was sure that he heard something inside of him snap as he dragged her to him.

HIS MOUTH crushed hers. The kiss wasn't loverlike. It was hard, demanding, and Natalie reveled in the onslaught of sensations sprinting through her. This was what she'd wanted, the mindless passion that only he could bring her. She could almost feel the barriers crumbling inside of her. He made her so aware of herself, so free.

No other man had ever made her feel this way. It was forbidden. It was delightful.

Even as his mouth devoured her, his fast, clever hands were everywhere, molding, pressing, possessing. Pleasure, hot spiky arrows of it, pierced her at every contact point.

When he drew back, she was trembling. Then he dragged her close again. "You're mine." His voice was a harsh whisper in her ear. "Mine."

Mine. The word echoed in her head as his mouth returned to hers. She'd wanted this madness, craved it from the moment she'd opened the door and seen him standing there. Now, he gave her no time to think, to breathe—no time to orient herself or anticipate. He ran his hand up her thigh and slipped two fingers into her, and her hips bucked to meet his touch. When he began to move his hand, her body moved with him, her muscles bunching, straining until her release, hot and hard, rocked her system. Only then did he drag her beneath him and drive himself into her on the floor of the shower.

"Look at me."

Shuddering, breathless, she opened her eyes to him. Water poured down, but even through the mists, she could see his gaze—dark and fixed on hers. Her vision and her body were filled with him. Her whole world had narrowed to him. There was nothing that she would have refused him.

"Say my name," he said.

For a split second, she hesitated, trying to clear her mind enough to remember who she was supposed to be. But he'd stripped all of those women from her.

Swearing, he withdrew and thrust into her again. "Say my name."

"Chance," she said. And she knew that it was Natalie who'd said the word, Natalie who was giving herself to him.

He nodded even as he began to move.

Wrapping her legs and arms around him, she gave herself over to the ride.

11

WHEN NATALIE opened her eyes in the morning, she found herself staring at Chance's sleeping face. Even as her mind readjusted to reality, recalling the job, the danger, the events of the night before, she kept studying him.

In sleep, he looked different. There was a hint of vulnerability, a hint of the boy that was seldom there when he was awake. Both pulled at her, and she felt her heart take a slow tumble.

Not good, she thought, as she pressed a fist against her chest. She was pretty sure the heart gymnastics thing had nothing to do with hot, sweaty sex or fantasies about what went on in Victorian brothels.

Where had that one come from anyway? She'd never read a Victorian porn novel in her life. And she'd better remember that the Victorian scenario hadn't been the only fantasy going down here. This whole thing she was playing out with Chance was a fantasy. He didn't even know she was here. He thought he was with Rachel and Calli. He certainly had no idea that the woman who'd given herself to him in the shower and all last night had been Natalie.

Suddenly, she frowned. No, she hadn't given herself to Chance. The word *give* was too closely associated with the heart acrobatics. And Natalie Gibbs was much too smart to give her heart to anyone. Maybe Calli was that type. As for Rachel, well, Natalie hoped that any cousin of hers would be wiser than that. But at least Natalie knew the kind of heartbreak that came when you allowed yourself to take that long fast fall into love. She'd seen what could happen up close and personal. Love had left her parents pining for something they could never have. And love for her dead husband had killed her mother.

No. She was not going to even think about the *L* word. *L-O-V-E* was not in her vocabulary. But as she lay there staring at him, she felt the little flutter near her heart begin again. Panic bubbled up. She had to get away from him to think.

After easing herself off the bed, she tiptoed backward to the closet, grabbed shorts, sandals and a shirt, then slipped as quietly as she could from the room.

SHE WAS GONE. Chance stood in the bathroom and struggled to keep panic at bay. When he'd woken up in an empty bed, he'd assumed she was in the bathroom. Their clothes were still lying where they'd dropped them, and her damn scent was still there. But there was no sign of Natalie. After moving out onto the balcony, he let his gaze sweep the grounds below. Relief streamed through him when he spotted her hurrying off in the direction of the beach.

Relief was pushed out by anger as he moved back into the bedroom for his clothes. What in the hell was she doing going off by herself? He dragged on trousers and pulled a shirt off of a hanger. They had roles to play, a job to do.

The next emotion to sweep over him was guilt. He should be lecturing himself on that score. Obviously, she was upset by what had happened between them during the night. Facing himself in the mirror, he tucked in the shirt and slipped into shoes. He could see the reflection of the bathroom door and the shower beyond. What had happened in there and later when he'd carried her into the bedroom had nothing to do with the masquerade they were involved in—or the job. He'd let his hormones take over.

No, that wasn't the whole truth. Placing his hands on the dresser, Chance leaned forward and met the eyes of the man staring back at him. Self-deception was not something that he'd ever let himself indulge in. It hadn't been merely hormones that had made him leave the poker game early. It had been feelings—feelings that he couldn't name, let alone sort out.

And he'd been swamped by feelings again in the shower. Calli, Rachel, Natalie—all three of them had gotten to him. But in the end it had been Natalie he'd made love to. Natalie he'd dragged to the floor. Natalie he'd demanded say his name. He was certain of that.

What he wasn't certain of was who Natalie had been making love to. Was it all role-playing for her? That was the question that he wanted to ask her, and it was not the question that should be foremost in his mind.

It was the job that should have his undivided attention.

Chance straightened and headed toward the bathroom. When he'd convinced Natalie to come with him to Brancotti's estate, she'd thought she'd be working with a professional. He'd have to make sure that she was. Until they had the Ferrante diamond and were safely off the estate, he had to find a way to stop touching her.

But even as the thought went through his head, he knew that keeping his hands off Natalie would be next to impossible.

SHE WASN'T ACTING like a professional. Natalie admitted that to herself as she reached the water. The sunlight glinted off the surface so intensely that she lifted a hand to shade her eyes. The quiet water and light breeze signaled that the day would be hot. The one thing that she'd always prided herself on was that she never let anything interfere with a job.

But last night, they'd…for the life of her, she wasn't sure what name to put to what they'd done to each other in that shower. All she was sure of was that when she'd seen Chance standing there in the doorway, she'd forgotten all about the job. All she could think of was having him.

Shoving down a fresh bubble of panic, she turned and started up the beach. What she needed was a bit of time to analyze what had happened. More importantly, who had allowed it to happen. From the time she was a child, she'd always loved pretending to be someone else. Her sisters had always enjoyed playing dress-up too, but for her it had always been about more than putting on outfits. She loved the whole process of getting into another person's psyche. For as long as he'd lived with them, her father had always encouraged her to develop her skill for what he called "slipping into other people."

With a dry laugh, she angled her path closer to the shoreline. Well, she'd "slipped" into some doozies last night. And the worst of it was, she'd enjoyed it. Never in her life had she felt so uninhibited, so wanton, so desirable. It had been wonderfully exciting until—

The cry of a gull had her shading her eyes and looking out over the water again. The white bird contrasted sharply with the wide expanse of blue sky. It called out again as it soared higher.

Freedom, Natalie thought. "Slipping into other people" offered her the freedom to escape from herself. Oh, she was her father's daughter all right. But last night she hadn't been able to completely carry off the charade. In the end, it had been Natalie who'd made love with Chance—in the shower and again in the bed. And…she'd lost a part of herself.

Stumbling, she pressed a hand against the tension in her stomach. Hadn't she known from the first time she'd looked into his eyes that he could touch her as no other man could?

It wasn't just the sex. It never had been just about the sex. That was why she hadn't been able to get him out of her mind for three months. That was why she'd decided to don a disguise for her next encounter with him. She'd done it to protect herself and it hadn't worked.

Natalie increased her pace and moved toward a part of the beach where tall grasses edged closer to the shore. She just needed to think. To plan. Choosing a spot near a lone palm tree, she sat down, drew her knees up and wrapped her arms around them.

What in the world was she going to do about Chance Mitchell? With a sigh, she rested her head on her knees. She supposed the answer to that question was simple and quite out of her hands. In a few days, the job would be over, Chance would go off to work on another case, and she would revert to being Detective Natalie Gibbs. Everything would return to normal, except that the job she'd loved for the past three years no longer held any appeal for her.

With one hand she scooped up white sand and let it flow through her fingers as she considered another question. Who was Natalie Gibbs? A part of her was her father's daughter, someone who loved dressing up and accepting the call to adventure. But she'd never before tried to analyze just what that said about who she was as a person. Why did she need to escape into other people? Or were they really "other people?" Just how much of Natalie Gibbs was in the people she slipped into? She scooped up more sand. There was a lot of her in the Rachel she'd created, and probably more of her than she'd thought in Calli. And if parts of her really were those other women, then did she know who she was at all?

Natalie wished that her father was with her so that she could talk to him about it. It wasn't often that she allowed herself to wish for him. At eleven, a year after he'd walked away from them, she'd locked those feelings away. For the sake of her sisters and her mother, she'd had to be strong and in control. But every so

often, the need and the emptiness slipped past her
guard and filled her as they did now. Even if her father couldn't tell her what to do, surely he could sym-
pathize. Had he ever wondered who he was?

SWEARING UNDER his breath, Chance jogged along the
beach. In the time it had taken him to get down the
stairs and out of the villa, Natalie had disappeared
from his view again. The moment he found her, they
were going to have a talk, and he was going to get her
word that she wouldn't go off by herself again.

Then he saw her, sitting with her head on her knees,
her shoulders slumped and he increased his pace immediately. Something was wrong. Natalie never sat
like that, and for that matter, neither did Rachel or
Calli. He thought of the woman he'd squared off with
on that mat in the Meridian's gym. She hadn't given
an inch. He thought of the woman he'd been with last
night, the woman who'd matched each of his demands
with one of her own.

Something was definitely wrong. Quickening his
pace, he knew the minute that she sensed his presence.
Her shoulders stiffened and she lifted her head. But her
gaze remained fixed on the water as if she needed a
moment to gather herself.

When he reached her, neither of them spoke. He
wanted to reach out a hand and stroke her hair, but once
he touched her, he wasn't sure he could stop touching her.

"You shouldn't go off like this on your own," he finally said.

Then she did look at him, and there was nothing of
the sadness that he'd sensed in her posture.

"I needed to think." With a smile, she patted the sand at her side. "And we need to talk."

She was Rachel. Chance was as certain of that as he was that she'd been Natalie when she'd been sad. Suddenly, he wanted the role-playing to stop. He wanted to talk to Natalie, find out what was bothering her.

But telling her now that he'd known all along that she was really Natalie Gibbs could put their whole job in jeopardy. Oh, she'd help him steal the Ferrante diamond. But there wasn't a doubt in his mind that Natalie would hate him for deceiving her. And Carlo Brancotti was good at reading people. Even the subtlest change in the relationship between Calli and Steven Bradford might make him suspicious.

"We'll have to be quick." She glanced past him down the beach. "I doubt that we'll be allowed to be here alone for very long. And I want to tell you where I think the safe is."

Chance cursed himself under his breath. As usual, she had her mind focused on the job. He didn't. Chance tabled the war going on inside of him. Now wasn't the time for his personal problems, but there was one thing he could do.

He took her hands. "I was too rough with you last night. You drove me crazy. I'm sorry."

Her eyes widened in surprise. "You don't have to apologize." Then she smiled, and he caught a glimpse of that light in her eyes that was so characteristic of Natalie. Chance once again found himself stifling the urge to grip her by the shoulders and tell her that he knew who she was.

Leaning forward, she brushed her lips against his. "I wasn't very gentle with you either."

Her scent filled him and sent images tumbling into his mind.

"I could be gentle." The words were a whisper against his skin, and then she used her tongue to trace his lips. "I could be very gentle if that's what you'd like."

Chance had slipped his hands into her hair and was about to take control of the kiss when he realized that it was happening again. All she had to do was touch him this way, and every other thought shot out of his mind.

He set her firmly away from him. "I think that until we get the diamond, we'd better keep totally focused on the job."

"I can multitask."

"I…" Chance paused for a second as he recalled just how good she was at multitasking. Then he cleared his throat. "I'm not as good, I'm afraid. It's not you. You're…" He paused again, battling both anger with himself and frustration. "Hell, yes it *is* you. You…distract me, and I want it to stop. I've waited a long time to get Brancotti. Can you understand that?"

"Yes." Natalie studied him through narrowed eyes. She thought she understood a great deal more than what he was saying. He'd spent one night with Natalie and disappeared for three months. Then he'd spent one night with Rachel and turned all business.

Now, he'd spent a day and a night with Calli, and he was all set to run for the hills again.

Chance raked a hand through his hair. "We can pretend we've had a fight. You've run away to the beach and I've followed. That will give us an excuse to keep our distance, and tonight I'll sleep on the couch in our room."

Not going to happen, she thought. This time, she was going to have something to say about it. She had a hunch all three of the women inside of her would.

"Do you turn tail and run every time you have great sex?" she asked.

"No." There was shock in his eyes, followed by a frown. "What are you talking about?"

Keeping her eyes steady on his, she leaned back against the palm tree. "Well, you spent one night with me when I was Rachel and backed off. Now, you've spent a day and a night with Calli and you're ready to back off again. My cousin Natalie never said you were a coward."

His gaze narrowed. "I'm not. I'm concerned about the job. Don't tell me that you aren't having some of the same misgivings. Otherwise, why would you have run away down here to think?"

In spite of the jitters in her stomach, she raised her brows and sent him a cool look. "Sure, I came out here to think and, yes, I find you distracting, too. But not enough to change our game plan. We've set up Steven and Calli as lovers who are passionately involved and just a bit unpredictable. Tonight at the masquerade ball, I figure we're going to need an excuse to slip away together so that we can pin down the location of the safe. Sex is something that Brancotti understands, and we've laid the foundation for it." She reached over to pat his hand. "Stop worrying about the sex and let's concentrate on getting the diamond. I think I know where the safe is."

"He showed you his office?"

"Twice. When he finished showing me the gardens, he let me into the house through the wing where he keeps his 'workspace.' He didn't take me inside, but he made sure I saw the coded keypad."

"That's where the diamond is?"

She shook her head. "That's where he wants me to think it is."

Chance frowned. "Then you think he suspects you?"

She rolled her eyes at him. "Well, yeah. We're in a room where we can't even talk to one another unless we go in the bathroom and turn on the shower." She shrugged. "But I think he suspects everyone."

"Okay. So why don't you believe that the diamond is behind the door with a keypad lock?"

"Because of a couple of things. One, he's a man who believes that he's smarter than anyone else and constantly likes to prove that. And two, he told me himself that he likes playing games."

"So?"

"Well, I've been thinking. What if showing me the room with the coded keypad was just a bit of game-playing—or misdirection, if you'd rather call it that? Then because he's so smart and his ego is enormous, he couldn't resist showing me the room where he *really* keeps the things that are most precious to him."

"Where?" Chance asked.

"There's a small art gallery down the hall from the main salon where he keeps his collection of paintings.

He told me he's going to hold the auction there, and I think the diamond is in a safe in that room."

Chance thought for a minute. "It would be just like him to pull something like that. He's always been a risk-taker, and I agree that he's a game-player. In fact, he could have a diamond in both places—a fake in one safe and the Ferrante diamond in the other." He met her eyes. "Unless we get lucky on the first try, we'll have to break into both safes."

Natalie's eyes gleamed. "Yeah. That's the way I figure it, too."

"How many paintings are in the gallery?"

"Ten."

"Ten paintings…I don't suppose you have any idea which one the safe is behind?"

Natalie smiled. "Did I say I thought it was behind a painting? I think he's a bit trickier than that. I'm betting it's concealed behind a panel in one of the pillars. He stood right in front of one of them, and I got this… feeling." She rubbed the back of her neck.

"How sure are you about this?"

A small frown appeared on her forehead. "It's a hunch. But I'm sure enough that I'm going to lure you into that room tonight and seduce you. You'll have to take care of the camera. Then I want to poke around those pillars."

"How long will you need?" Chance asked.

"As much time as you can get me."

He raised her hand and pressed his lips against her fingers. "You're very good at this game of deception we're playing."

She gave him a quick glance and caught the intent

look in his eyes. For one moment, she wondered if he knew that she wasn't Rachel Cade.

"We'd better get back to the house," she said.

Chance didn't move. He merely studied her for a moment. He might be losing his focus, but she wasn't losing hers. He was very glad that he'd brought her to Florida with him.

"Carlo is going to wonder if we don't get back," she said.

"Let him," Chance said as he remembered the way she'd looked when he'd first seen her here on the beach. "Let's go wading first."

"Wading?"

The surprise on her face pleased him. "You take your shoes off and walk in the water."

"I'm familiar with the concept. I just don't get the purpose."

The dryness in her tone had him shooting her a sideways glance. "Fun. Once we go back to the house, we're Calli and Steven. Right now, we can be whoever we want. Didn't you ever skip school and play hooky as a kid?"

"No."

Chance grinned at her. It was his Natalie who'd answered. He was certain of it. "No. Of course not."

Her chin lifted. "And you played hooky a lot?"

"You might say that my early life was pretty much one long game of hooky." He walked to the shoreline, toed his shoes off and then leaned down to take off his socks.

"How so?" she asked, kicking off her sandals and joining him.

"It's a long story," Chance said.

"I can wade and listen at the same time," Natalie pointed out.

They began to walk. The sun beat down on their shoulders and arms, and the lukewarm water lapped at their ankles. "My mother moved around a lot, mostly within London and the south of England. But a few times, she followed a band to Scotland or Wales. She was what you would call in America a groupie—and she was especially fond of young groups that were just starting out. Sometimes, they'd give her work, repairing and laundering costumes or passing out flyers. I got to help with that."

Natalie frowned as she slipped her hand into his. "She took you with her?"

"She was only sixteen when I was born, and she didn't have any family. Most of the time she supported the two of us by waitressing. She thought that was the best kind of job because she could bring home food. Plus, it was something that she could do just as well in one town as another."

Chance shot her a look and saw that the frown had deepened on her face. "It wasn't as bad as it sounds. She was pretty and she laughed a lot. And she loved me. It wasn't until I got to the orphanage that I started to go to school regularly."

"Orphanage?"

Chance shrugged. He rarely let himself think about that part of his life, and he never talked about it. He wasn't sure why he was now except that what they were doing reminded him in a way of that early part of his life before the orphanage. "One night she never came home. Police came to the door the next morning. She'd been struck by a bus on her way home from a concert."

Natalie simply turned and wrapped her arms around him. "I'm sorry. How old were you?"

"Twelve." Chance found that it was hard to get the word out because once again feelings were swamping him. He felt his body stiffen, not in defense but in surprise. There was none of the fire that he usually felt when she held him. In its place was a steady warmth and a sweetness that seemed to squeeze his heart. Her head was pressed against his chest, her arms wrapped around him, and he could have stood like this, just like this for a very long time.

Slipping a finger beneath her chin, he lifted it because he had to see her eyes. He could see sympathy and affection and a question.

"Chance?"

He wanted more than anything to kiss her. To lower his head, press his mouth to hers and lose himself in her. But if he did, he knew he would lose something that he would never get back. At the last second he set her away from him.

She turned away, but not before he saw the hurt in her eyes. He had his mouth open, his hand outstretched when he realized that the name in his mind, on his lips, was *Natalie*.

He barely had time to swallow it when he heard the crack and felt the burning sting in his shoulder. The next shot hit the wet sand not three feet from them.

"Run." Grabbing her hand, Chance fixed his gaze on the line of palms half a football field away and dragged her with him.

12

NATALIE STRUGGLED to swallow her fear as they raced for the cover of the trees. Sand sprayed up less than a yard to their right, and Chance's grip on her arm tightened. "Sprint."

Fighting to keep her breathing even, she felt the pull in her calves each time her foot sank into the sand and struggled for traction. Fifty yards became forty…thirty…twenty. There was another spray of sand, this one to her left. Finally, they reached the first line of trees.

Chance kept up the pace until palm leaves closed in on them and the sand at their feet became completely covered over with vegetation. Beach had become swamp in an instant. They would have to go more slowly now or run the risk of falling or twisting an ankle.

"Follow me," Chance said. It was only when he took the lead that Natalie saw the blood on his shirt.

"You've been hit."

Chance pulled the shirt off his shoulder and glanced down at the wound. "It's just a scratch. C'mon."

Natalie pressed a hand against the knot of fear that had formed in her stomach. The mark was angry-looking and it was oozing blood. But he was right, she told herself. It was just a scratch. And she wasn't going to let herself think about the fact that it might have been worse.

They walked swiftly in silence for a while. Natalie tried to keep her mind blank and focus on putting one foot in front of another. Moving as fast as he could, Chance cut a path through the vegetation by tamping down palm fronds and grasses. Now only thin spears of sunlight pierced the darkening gloom, and damp heat pressed in on them. Natalie felt a trickle of sweat run down her neck.

Something moved under her foot. Stifling a scream, Natalie reached out to grab a fistful of Chance's shirt.

"What?" He stopped and turned so fast that she bumped into him.

"Nothing," she said.

When he merely studied her for a minute, she lifted her chin and repeated, "Nothing. Go."

She was just not going to let herself think of what might be under her bare feet, not while a gunman might be after them. Snakes had always scared her, but they weren't nearly as dangerous as whoever was using them for rifle practice.

"This way," Chance said and made a sharp right turn.

She hoped he knew where he was going, because the oval expanse of black water to her left had her thinking of another kind of danger that lurked in the Florida swamps. Alligators. Hadn't she read that wherever there was water, you could bank on finding one— or more?

No. She tore her gaze away from the water, fastened

her eyes on Chance's back and made herself think about who had shot at them. Brancotti? Had he somehow seen through their disguises? But how?

If it wasn't Brancotti, who else could it be? Keeping her gaze fastened on Chance's back, she pictured each one of the people she'd met at the dinner party the previous night.

Her favorite suspect would have to be Armand Genovese. A man with mob connections wouldn't even have to pull the trigger himself. He'd have easy access to a professional hit man.

And a hit man wouldn't give up until the job was done. He might even now be following them into the swamp.

Natalie risked one quick glance over her shoulder and saw only shadows. She stumbled, caught herself and refocused her attention on Chance's back.

Sir Arthur probably hunted, but even when she formed an image of him with a rifle in his hands, she found it hard to believe that he was a killer.

She didn't know as much about the other guests, but they were all very wealthy. Any one of them could have hired someone.

But why would any of them want to kill Steven— unless…

Chance stopped abruptly, and she walked smack into him again. Peering over his shoulder, she saw the trunk of a fallen palm tree blocking their path. He gripped her hand and guided her around it.

Once on the other side, they crouched down and Chance leaned close, his voice making no more sound than a breath. "If we're being followed…" He reached into his pocket and drew out a small gun. Together, they waited, listening. Gradually, she could hear other sounds above their breathing. No sounds of footsteps. Leaves rustled overhead, insects buzzed, and farther off, a gull shrieked. A minute stretched into two and then three. Natalie shivered as she watched a spider the size of her fist crawl down the side of the tree trunk.

Clamping her teeth together, she made herself wait another minute before she said, "I want to get out of here."

"Yes," Chance said. "'Calli' can get sick. I'll tell Brancotti that I want to fly you back to New York."

She stared at him. "Forget it. I was talking about getting out of this swamp. I'm not leaving you here alone."

His expression was grim, his eyes cold. "It's too dangerous. I don't want you here."

"Tough." She could make her eyes cold, too. "I don't cut and run until a job is finished. Besides, you need my help."

He said nothing for a minute. Because she was right. Natalie pressed her advantage. "We've decided that unless we get lucky and find the real diamond on the first try, we have to hit both safes. You won't be able to do that alone. Once the job is done, I'll be ready to leave. And instead of arguing with me, you'd best put your energy into figuring out who took that shot at us."

CHANCE SHOVED DOWN on the emotions that had been swirling through him since they'd narrowly missed that barrage of bullets on their sprint for the trees. He couldn't afford to let them cloud his mind, not now when he had to focus on protecting Natalie. Gathering his thoughts, he said, "I don't have to figure anything out. It was Brancotti."

She shook her head. "Not necessarily. It could be anyone he's invited to his house party."

Chance bit back his impatience as she ran through her little rogue's gallery of suspects, but he still wasn't convinced. "What's their motivation?"

"Any one of them could be worried that Steven Bradford might outbid them."

Chance shook his head. "My money's still on Brancotti."

"He's a businessman. He wants Steven Bradford here as competition. You'll drive the price up."

She had a sharp mind. Chance had to admit that, but she wasn't aware of all of the facts. "I've gone up against him before."

"I read the file. You lost your partner."

Chance nodded. "He could have put us in the Venetian room to let me know that he suspects who I really am. And now he's decided that the game is over."

Natalie thought for a minute. "I don't think so. Wouldn't he rather play the game out to the finish—let you get the diamond in your hand and then spring a trap?"

Chance remained silent. She could almost see his mind at work.

"Besides, if he kills Steven Bradford, he calls attention to this place. He can't want the police wandering through, questioning his guests or even worse, wondering why all these people are gathered here. It's too risky."

"But he didn't kill me," Chance pointed out. "He could still intend to play the game to the finish. Either way, it's too risky for you to stay."

Natalie studied him in silence for a moment. Then she said, "I'm not going unless you come with me."

"I'm not leaving without the Ferrante diamond."

"Then I stay, too."

Chance grabbed her wrist as she started to rise. "Haven't you heard a word I've said? It's too dangerous for you to stay. It's possible that Brancotti set this whole auction up to trap me because I came too close to catching him the last time."

She gave him a long, cool look, and when she spoke, her voice was just as chilly. "I've heard everything you said. But I don't desert my partners."

When he opened his mouth, she raised a hand to silence him. "You haven't convinced me yet that Carlo is on to us. Your history with him and the fact that you lost a partner may be clouding your judgment."

"You may be right, but—" He cut himself off as he looked into those cop's eyes. He owed her the rest of the truth. "There's more that I haven't told you. Carlo and I go back a long way—all the way back to that orphanage I told you about. His name was Damien back then, and he was my best friend, my mentor. I trusted him until he betrayed me."

"How?" Natalie asked.

"I was twelve and he was seventeen when I was placed there, and he took me under his wing right from the start. You've seen what he's like. I came to worship him. The nuns at the orphanage trusted him, too. He could go anywhere without being questioned.

He had a knack for opening locks and under his tutoring I found that I did, too. After lights-out at night, he'd come and get me, and we'd practice. Once a month they changed the combination on the safe in the headmistress's office. Damien would finesse the lock on her office door and then we'd practice on the safe. It took a while, but eventually, I was able to open it. Each month after that we'd have competitions to see who could open it the fastest."

Natalie couldn't help but recall that she and her father had had the same kind of competitions.

"One night, Damien excused himself while I was working on the safe. He said he had a surprise for me. I don't know how long he was gone. I was totally focused on listening to the tumblers fall. This particular night the safe was empty. I didn't even have time to wonder about that when Damien returned with the headmistress and the police. There'd been over a hundred thousand dollars in the safe—money from the annual fund-raiser. Looking back, I can see that Damien had laid his plans far in advance."

"They didn't suspect him?" Natalie asked.

Chance laughed dryly. "Why would anyone suspect St. Damien? He looked as horrified as the headmistress to find me there. He told them that he'd heard something when he was making his rounds and he'd called the police immediately. They found me in front of the open safe, and then they found letters under my mattress—from my accomplice. In them, I was told just what to do and I was even given the combination of the safe. The police assumed that I had tossed the money out the open window of the office to my 'partner' and that, thanks to Damien, I hadn't had time to make my escape. Looking back, I can see how stupid I was."

"You were twelve, a child. How could they have been so stupid to suspect you?"

Chance glanced down to find that Natalie had slipped her hand into his. He couldn't help wondering how his life might have turned out if someone at the orphanage had had even a little of that simple faith in him. "The nuns didn't think that being twelve was an excuse. And they didn't want to disbelieve Damien."

"What did they do with you?" she asked.

"I was taken away to jail. Of course, my accomplice was never found. Later, I learned that Damien left the orphanage shortly after that."

"And no one suspected even then?"

Chance shook his head, almost smiling at the vehemence in her tone. "He was close to eighteen, and he had a right to leave."

"What happened to you?" she asked.

Chance smiled. "Don't look so worried. The one thing I owed Damien for was that I'd become very good with locks. I spent one night in the town jail before I blew the place."

"You were twelve and alone on the streets?"

Because he couldn't resist her, he briefly touched his lips to hers. "The streets were a hell of a lot better than that jail. Now that you know what Carlo is really like, is there any chance that I can convince you to leave?"

"No."

There were some battles you could win, Chance thought, and some you retreated from so that you could fight another day. Tipping up her chin, he met her eyes steadily. "We're going to have to be very careful."

"Yes, we'll need some kind of a plan."

Chance could almost hear the wheels inside her head turning.

She glanced around. "I'll be able to think better once we get out of this place. If there's one creature that scares me more than alligators and snakes, it's spiders."

Laughing, Chance tucked his gun away, then pulled her to her feet and said, "Follow me."

"HAVE YOU GOT IT?" Natalie asked.

Chance glanced down at her as they stepped onto the circular drive that led to the house. There were smudges of dirt on her nose and cheeks, but she was totally focused on explaining the tack she thought they ought to take with Brancotti. It wasn't bad as plans went, Chance supposed.

"I'm going to be upset, angry, afraid," she said. "Someone shot at us, and I'm going to want answers."

Natalie Gibbs was a woman who seldom lost her focus, except when he was making love with her. Then that line of concentration disappeared from her brow, and that incredible mist would fill her eyes and darken them.

"Well?"

He filed away the image that had filled his mind and glanced down at her.

"And you're going to be—?" she prompted.

"I'm going to be upset and withdrawn. Let you take control. I don't much like that part."

She shot him a grin. "Steven Bradford's a bit of a weenie. That makes him very sexy to someone like me."

"I'll have to remember that," Chance said.

"I'd rather that you remember the plan—and stick to it."

He'd stick to it for a while, at least. Their best shot at leaving the estate with the diamond was to continue playing their roles. Natalie's instincts were good, and she was managing to keep her objectivity a hell of a lot better than he was. For the moment, he couldn't do better than to follow her lead.

"Ready?" she asked as they climbed the steps.

"Yeah. Are you ready?"

"Yes." She drew in a deep breath, let it out. And then Chance watched her turn into Calli.

Her step quickened and she slipped her hand into his. "The first thing I'm going to do is demand that you see a doctor."

"Whoa. That wasn't part of the plan you just outlined. I don't need a doctor," he said. "It's just a scratch."

"It's bleeding. A doctor should look at it."

She was being mother hen, Chance thought in some disgust. There was a lot of Natalie, the big sister, in Calli.

They stepped into the entrance hall just as Lisa entered from one of the hallways.

"I demand to see Carlo," Natalie cried. "Someone just tried to kill Steven."

"This way," Lisa said, gesturing them into the hallway she'd just stepped out of. "Carlo has already been informed of the incident. He's talking to the security people right now."

Chance let Natalie draw him down the hallway. Lisa stopped at a door with a coded keypad. Figuring that this was the same room that Carlo had shown Natalie on her tour, he took a quick survey as he stepped through the door. He spotted the guard right away, just outside the doors that opened onto a patio. Natalie strode forward and placed her hands, palms down, on Carlo's desk. "What is going on here?"

Carlo glanced at Chance, then back at Natalie. "I'm working on it. My men are searching for the shooter. I hope to hear shortly that they have apprehended him."

"And why should we trust you?" Natalie asked. "How can we be sure that it wasn't one of your men who shot Steven?"

For a moment there was silence in the room as Carlo looked from Natalie to Chance and back again. Chance could see the anger in Carlo's eyes and in the pulse beating in his temple. For a moment, he wondered if Natalie had gone too far.

Finally, Carlo moved around his desk and took one of Natalie's hands. "You're upset. Understandably so. Please." He glanced at Chance and gestured to the two chairs in front of his desk. "Sit down. Lisa? Pour our guests some brandy."

As Lisa did his bidding, Natalie and Chance sat while Carlo picked up his phone and punched in numbers. "I'm calling my own personal doctor. She lives right here on the estate. You'll want to have the wound looked at."

"It's only a scratch," Chance said. "Give me some antiseptic and a Band-Aid and I'll be fine."

"Thank you. He'll see a doctor," Natalie said.

Carlo gave orders over the phone, then hung up and waited for Lisa to distribute the brandy snifters.

He took a quick sip of his before he spoke, and Chance used that moment to study his old enemy more closely. Carlo's hand wasn't quite steady as he set his glass down on the desk. He was either rattled or giving a good imitation of it. Of course, Chance was well aware that Carlo was skilled at deception.

But what would be the point of acting rattled? Unless he truly was. Was it possible that Natalie was right and Carlo wasn't behind the shooting?

Chance had no reason to give him the benefit of the doubt.

"I want to apologize." Carlo said. "Nothing like this has ever happened on my estate before. In answer to your earlier question, I don't usually invite people here to shoot them. This villa—" he gestured with a hand "—is a place where I conduct a very lucrative business. And most of my clients are repeat customers. If word got around that something like this could happen here…well, you can imagine the repercussions. That is why you may rest assured that I had nothing to do with this deplorable incident. You can also be certain that I will do everything in my power to get to the bottom of it."

It was a nice speech, Chance thought. There was a line of tension in Carlo's shoulders and a bite of fury in his movements as he lifted the glass and took another sip of brandy. It was a superb performance.

"You say the shooter isn't one of your men. But how could he have gotten past your security?" Natalie asked.

Bull's-eye, Chance thought as a muscle twitched in Carlo's jaw. Was that why Carlo was so angry?

"That is an excellent question. I will have the answer soon," he promised.

On impulse, Chance said, "I want to send Calli home."

She rounded on him. "No. If we go, we go together. I don't care about that diamond. I only care about you."

There were real tears in her eyes. Chance would have staked his life on it. And they hadn't discussed this scenario. He'd sprung it on her out of the blue.

"No. Please," Carlo said.

Ignoring him, Chance looked only at Natalie. "I can't put you in danger."

She reached for his hand. "I won't leave you here."

The phone on Carlo's desk rang. "Excuse me." He reached for it. "Yes?… I'll be there shortly." After replacing the handset, he said to them, "My security team has apprehended the shooter. I'll get to the bottom of this, I promise you. In the meantime, I want you to let my personal doctor look at the wound." He turned to Natalie. "I promise you that you will both be safe here. I don't want you to leave. I'll auction the diamond tonight."

Good, Chance thought. The sooner he got Natalie off the estate, the better.

Natalie kept her grip tight on Chance's hand. "Will you see the doctor?"

"Yes. All right," Chance agreed.

"Ah," Carlo said as a small round woman with gray hair and wire-framed glasses was ushered in. "Dr.

Canfield, I'd like you to meet Steven Bradford and his friend Calli. Steven has a bullet wound that I'd like you to take a look at."

"It's a scratch," Chance protested.

The woman stopped short and sent Carlo a stubborn look. "I have to report a bullet wound." Chance got the impression the outspoken woman wasn't afraid of anyone or anything.

"By all means," Carlo said. "I plan on making a report myself just as soon as I speak with my security team and find out why this unacceptable incident occurred."

"Just so we're straight." With a brief nod for Carlo, she bore down on Chance and set her black bag on the edge of the desk. Then she said to Calli, "Is he going to be a baby about this?"

Natalie raised her brows. "He's a man, so of course, he's going to be a baby."

Chance suspected Dr. Canfield was biting back a smile as she turned and opened her bag.

"I'm leaving you in good hands," Carlo said as he signaled Lisa to follow him out of the room.

13

"TWO THINGS." Natalie pitched her voice low, gesturing with the lollipop the doctor had given him as a joke after she'd dressed his wound. She sat cross-legged on the edge of the bathroom sink while he shaved. Behind them, the shower was thundering like Niagara Falls, so they could talk safely.

"First, I think the diamond might be in the safe in Carlo's office after all."

Chance let his razor pause in midstroke and shifted his gaze to Natalie. "Why?"

She paused for a moment to gather her thoughts, and a tiny line appeared on her forehead. Chance wondered if she was at all aware that she'd slipped into being Natalie. "Three reasons. Number one and two are related—the guard and the fact there was no camera in the room."

Chance continued to draw the razor down his cheek. She was good. There wasn't a second that they'd been in Carlo's office that he'd seen her attention waver from either Carlo or him, but she'd still managed to scan the room for recording devices. "It's not surprising that he wouldn't have a camera in his office. That's his private space. He wouldn't want someone even on his own security team seeing everything that goes on in there. Or overhearing everything he says on the phone."

"Yeah." She tapped the lollipop against her lips. "That's the way I figure it, too. But the presence of a guard could mean there's something very valuable in the safe to protect."

"Or the guard could be stationed there to protect Carlo."

She shook her head. "He didn't go with Carlo. He stayed in the room. I'm betting Lisa is Carlo's bodyguard as well as assistant. And I think she sleeps with him."

Chance shot her a questioning glance. That was something he hadn't noticed. "They're lovers?"

"I'd bet good money on it. There's something in the way that Lisa looks at him."

"Your third reason?" Chance rinsed his razor under the faucet.

She frowned. "It's harder to explain, but it goes back to games. You mentioned he's fond of misdirection. So at first, I thought that he showed me the office with the coded access pad to make me think the diamond's there when it's really in the gallery. But maybe it's the other way around—and he took me to the gallery to make me think it's there while it's in his office with a coded pad on one door and a guard stationed at the other. Does that make any sense?"

Chance nodded. "Perfect sense. But we'll still have to hit both safes."

Natalie sighed. "Agreed. But I think we should do the office first."

Chance said, "We'll see."

"We should have a definite plan."

"I'm working on it. You said two things. What else did you want to talk about?"

She straightened a bit and rotated her shoulders. "I'm more convinced than ever that Carlo wasn't behind the shooting."

"Be careful." Chance drew the razor on one final stroke along his jawline. "You're letting the man get to you again."

"No. But I do have to give him points for calling in his private doctor."

"Damage control. He doesn't want it to become public knowledge that guests on his estate run the risk of being shot. And you only liked her because she swabbed my shoulder with something that could take the finish off cars."

Her lips curved. "Don't be such a baby."

Chance took a towel off his good shoulder and wiped his face with it. "Remember, all of Brancotti's charm is on the surface. Underneath, he's as cold and ruthless as they come. And he's the most likely candidate. He knew we were both down on the beach—the security cameras would have shown him that. All he had to do was pick up a phone and give the order."

Natalie pulled the lollipop out of her mouth. "But he was rattled when we walked in the room. And furious."

"Because his men botched the job."

"Or because something happened on his estate that took him by surprise, something that he wasn't in control of. That would piss him off."

She had a point. He'd given it some thought himself, but he wasn't convinced. Chance studied her as he rinsed his razor under the running water. As she tucked a strand of hair behind her ear in a gesture that was pure Natalie, something tightened around his heart. When the job was done, he was going to miss working with her, pitting himself against the sharp mind of hers. He was going to miss her. Period.

"Carlo didn't like it at all when he thought we might leave." Pausing, she pointed the lollipop at him. "I didn't appreciate that little improvisation either. It wasn't part of the plan."

He shrugged. "I have trouble sticking to plans. I wanted to see his reaction." He recalled hers—the tears that had sprung to her eyes. Would she miss working with him? Miss him?

"Rachel…"

"Hmmmm?"

As she met his eyes, he watched that total concentration shift to him. If he told her the truth now—that he'd known all along she was Natalie Gibbs—he might be able to convince her to go.

"What is it?" she asked.

As he played with a strand of her hair, he knew that he wasn't going to tell her—for the same reason that he hadn't pushed the issue in Carlo's office. In spite of the danger, in spite of everything, he wanted her with him for as long as he could have her.

"I want you," he said.

The tiny line appeared on her forehead again. "We should nail down details for tonight."

"Okay." He hung up his towel and turned to her. It

was then that he noticed the line of dried blood on the top of her foot. "You didn't tell me that you were hurt."

She glanced down. "I'm not. It's just a scratch."

Chance plugged the sink and turned the faucets on. "That defense strategy didn't work for me." He paid no heed to her grumbled comments as he drew her feet into the water.

"Ouch."

"I thought it was only men who were babies." Ignoring her little huff of breath, he lifted the injured foot out of the water, placed the sole in the palm of his hand and began to massage soap gently over the scratch. It *was* merely a scratch, he discovered, but there was more than one.

"I can do that," she said.

"Yes," he agreed amiably as he slipped a soapy finger in and out between her toes. "But why don't you tell me what you believe would be a good plan for tonight?"

"I think we ought to…"

"Yes?" He ran a hand up her calf to the back of her knee.

"Since there are two safes…we should…"

Watching her, he moved his fingers up the inside of her thigh. "We're not sure there are two safes."

"There are. I'm sure…you're distracting me."

"Really?" He traced his fingers back down her calf and rinsed her foot. "You're the most focused person I know."

"Two safes…two people…the most…efficient way to handle it would be…"

Her last words had come out in a rush, Chance

noted as he lifted her foot and pressed his mouth to the scratch. He heard the quick catch of her breath. And when he turned, he saw the mix of desire and confusion in her eyes. It struck him then that he'd never once taken the time to seduce her. Oh, he'd made love to her, but it had always been fast and hot. Wonderful in its own way, but… He watched her eyes darken as he ran his tongue along the scratch, then took one quick nip at the arch of her foot.

"Chance, I…"

"You were saying that the most efficient way to handle it would be to…?" Lowering her foot, he leaned in and brushed his mouth over hers.

"I can't think when you…do that."

"How about this?" He traced her lips with his tongue. "You taste like cherry lollipop." Then he shifted his attention to her other foot. This time he ran his hand up to the inside of her thigh and let it linger there. "You were saying…?"

"You're making it…hard to think."

He was going to make it impossible. But he didn't say that. Instead, he traced little patterns on the inside of her thigh and savored the quick catch of her breath.

"Why are we always in such a hurry?" he asked.

Her lips were parted, moist and stained cherry-red. He leaned in for another sample. Heat shimmered. The moment it threatened to flare, he drew back.

"No." The plea came out on a sigh.

The sight of her, aroused and at his mercy, excited him in a way that hadn't happened before. Watching only her eyes, he skimmed his fingers higher up the inside of her thigh until he could touch the lace of her panties. This time he intended to go slowly. "Tell me more about your plan."

Natalie sucked in a breath and wished that she could gather her thoughts just as quickly. There was some important point that she had to make. But she couldn't quite grasp hold of it.

"Or you could just let me touch you," Chance said.

She shuddered as his fingers traced the lace on the edge of her panties. She waited, shuddering again in anticipation of when they would slip beneath the thin silk and enter her. But they didn't. They merely traced the same path over and over.

Sensations moved through her. And they were so new—nothing like the flash and fire he'd always ignited in her before. This was…softer…sweeter, and her blood felt as if it had turned thick as honey.

"I love the feel of your skin." His hand moved down the inside of her thigh to her knee and then slowly back again. He repeated the process on her other thigh.

She could have sworn that she was floating. Ridiculous. She was still sitting on the counter. She could feel the hard press of it against her bottom and the heels of her hands. But what Chance was doing to her with just his hands made her feel as if he'd magically levitated her several inches above the counter.

That was ridiculous. And she should put a stop to it. She opened her mouth, intending to do just that when he drew her feet out of the sink and shifted her so that her back was propped against the mirror and he was standing between her legs.

He pulled her shorts off and dropped them on the floor in one smooth move.

"Open your eyes."

She hadn't even been aware that she'd closed them, but she did as he asked. She would have done anything he asked.

"I want to touch you here." He ran one finger down the silk of her panties until it rested against the center of her heat.

She shuddered as a wave of pleasure pierced her, weakening her. Helpless to do anything else, she watched him, waiting, wanting.

For a moment, he didn't move at all. And she couldn't. Everything inside of her was melting.

"Please…"

His finger moved then, but only to trace the same erotic patterns he'd made earlier on her thigh.

"No…please." Gathering all of her strength, she arched toward him, craving more.

He drew his hand away, gripped her thighs and pulled her to the edge of the counter. Then leaning down, he began to trace the same pattern on the silk of her panty with his tongue.

Pleasure built to a knife-edged pain inside of her as she strained toward him. But she couldn't get close enough, and he kept the pressure so gentle. Too gentle. The torture was so exquisite, she thought she might die of it.

"I can't… Please."

He drew her panties off then and followed their path down her legs with his mouth. Then he began the journey back up. If she'd thought she might die before, Natalie was quite sure she would now as sensation after sensation battered through her. There was the scrape of his teeth at her ankle, the slick pressure of his tongue on her calf, and the string of kisses that drew closer and closer, only to stop before they reached their goal.

And then his mouth was just where she wanted it to be, and the pressure was just what she'd been craving. She called out his name as the orgasm erupted. His arms were around her as the pleasure careened through her with a force that built and built and built to a high, airless peak. As she shot over it, all she knew was Chance.

And then he was inside of her, moving slowly in and out, in and out. She couldn't feel anymore. She was sure of it, but then the heat started to build again. And still he went slowly, too slowly. Drawing on all of her strength, she wrapped herself around him and began to move. She knew the moment the pleasure built to the flash point for him, and she went with him into the fire.

"WHAT DO YOU THINK of the costume?"

Natalie stared at herself in the mirror and tried to think of an appropriate Calli response. Of course, Chance had sprung the costume on her out of the blue.

And they still didn't have a decent plan. Once she'd managed to gather up her brain cells after they'd made love, she'd suggested that they split up and each break into one of the safes. He'd rejected it, but what he'd replaced it with was sketchy at best. The only thing she was sure of was that they were going to break into the gallery safe first. In her mind, the sketchy details meant that he intended to improvise.

"Great, aren't they?"

Natalie dragged her focus back to the costumes. The fact that they were in the bedroom and being listened to kept her from saying what she really thought about them. She shifted her gaze to Chance's reflection in the mirror. He was Stan Laurel. Tall and lean, he looked the part right up to the dopey expression on his face. Very cute.

She, on the other hand, was a fat, pudgy and very disgruntled Oliver Hardy. Spikey little black bangs peeked out from the bowler hat she was wearing, and she had a mustache and chipmunk cheeks. Chance had made her stuff cotton rolls in them.

Finally, she let her gaze drift down to the stomach that felt as big as Kansas. The added padding around her middle held her tools and a second costume just in case they had to improvise at some point in the evening.

Just in case they had to improvise? Yeah, right. But she felt better knowing that at least Chance had some sort of a backup plan. Still, the added girth around her middle was going to slow her down.

"You really look like Oliver Hardy," Chance said, grinning at her.

She did. And Calli should have some reaction to that. Someone was listening, but her mind had gone suddenly blank. How would Calli feel about wearing this costume?

For some reason she'd been finding it harder to keep in character since they'd made love in the bathroom. She was pretty sure that the clutch of nerves in her stomach had more to do with the way that Chance had made her feel than the job they had to do tonight.

"I was sure you'd like it," Chance said.

Stalling, she fisted her hands on her hips and focused on her image in the mirror. But she didn't want to be Calli right now. And she didn't want to be Rachel Cade either. What she really wanted was to drag Chance back in the bathroom and ask him what he'd meant by making her feel the way he had.

He'd made her feel loved. The word had fear and panic slithering up her spine, but it was better to get it out and face it than to let it gnaw away at her.

He'd made her feel something that wasn't real, that she couldn't have. Better to get that harsh truth out and face it, too. Maybe then, she could get her mind back on the job they had to do.

"You love watching my collection of Oliver and Hardy films…" The expression on Chance's face was puzzled. He'd probably looked forward to throwing her this curve ball, Natalie thought.

Tilting her head to one side, she met his eyes and said, "Loving the films doesn't mean I want to dress up like them. And I don't see why I have to be the fat guy."

Chance grinned Stan Laurel's silly grin and flipped his tie at her. "Because I'm taller."

She rolled her eyes and ad-libbed. "I never should have let you pick out the costumes."

"You told me to pick a couple."

"I was thinking of a couple couple. Romeo and Juliet, Antony and Cleopatra…" Switching her gaze to her own image in the mirror, she frowned. "I think I ought to get a reward for wearing this."

He reached for her hand and raised it to his lips. "By

the end of the evening, you'll have the Ferrante diamond. You can bank on it."

She met his eyes then. "I will." And that was all she was going to think about for the rest of the evening— getting her hands on that diamond.

"Ready?" Chance asked.

The ringing of his cell phone prevented her from replying.

"Yes, Harold," Chance said.

It was Tracker checking in again. He would have facts and figures to give Steven on the latest merger that Bradford Enterprises was engaged in. Sandwiched in would be anything important that Tracker wanted Chance to know.

While she waited, Natalie checked herself one more time in the mirror and practiced walking back and forth.

"There's been a little shooting incident," Chance said. "Nothing serious, but you can cancel the fishing trip and expect me back in New York tomorrow morning."

Nicely done, Natalie thought. Now, Tracker would know that they had to leave the island tonight. Once Chance pocketed his phone, he turned toward her and handed her one of the feathery masks that Carlo had provided. "Ready?"

She felt her heart flip and tried to ignore it. This was a man who would never be hers, but they were about to embark on the adventure of a lifetime. This was why she'd signed on. Later, she'd test her ability to deal with a wounded heart. Right now, she was going to trust in her ability to pull off this job.

"Ready," she said and waddled toward him.

14

OVER THE TOP. That was the phrase that popped into Natalie's mind the minute she walked into the main salon. Carlo had brought the room to life as surely as if he'd been the prince who'd awakened Sleeping Beauty. Crystal chandeliers glimmered overhead, and the wall of French doors stood open to the night. Across the room, tables draped in white linen cloths held silver buckets of champagne and trays of food. And there were flowers everywhere, their scents blending with candle wax and expensive perfume. A band played in the far corner of the dance floor, and she noted that the room was already more than half-filled with people.

Carlo Brancotti's masquerade ball was *the* party to be invited to in South Florida. She'd almost forgotten that, and as Natalie let her gaze sweep the room, she wondered how many politicians and other assorted celebrities hid behind the glittering, feathery masks that Carlo had provided. It was a night to pretend, to do things you might not if you were yourself.

That's what she was going to focus on. Taking a deep breath, she waddled at Chance's side as they stepped into the line that was filing past Carlo and

Lisa. Carlo's assistant wore a blond wig and a long, white dress, glittering with sequins. Barbie, Natalie guessed.

But Carlo didn't resemble the rather preppy-looking Ken. He wore a tuxedo with the same flair and effect as James Bond. With his long hair pulled back and fastened with a gold clip at the back of his neck, and one diamond glinting in his ear, he looked to be what he was—a rich, powerful man. There was nothing on the surface to even hint at the ruthless lowlife beneath.

"Ah, the film celebrities…" He paused and turned to Lisa. "Let me present Oliver Hardy and Stan Laurel." As Chance took Lisa's hand, Carlo continued, "And my companion, Barbie."

Natalie was sure that Carlo recognized her when he took her hand. And she also noted that he wore a tiny listening device in his ear—a clever way to get updates from his security people. The moment they were out of earshot, she nudged Chance and spoke in a tone only he could hear. "He's got a receiver in his ear."

"And a microphone in his tie. He hasn't survived this long without being very cautious. Want to try the food?"

"No, thanks." She patted her stomach. "Right now, it's pretty jammed up with nerves."

"Then, we'll dance."

"Dance?" she asked as he drew her onto the dance floor.

"Yes. I take your hand, like this, and I put my other hand at your waist, like this."

"I understand the concept—but we're two men."

"It's a masquerade," he said as he guided her

smoothly into the rhythm of the music. "Anything goes."

"This is ridiculous," she said.

"No," Chance murmured as he steered her down the length of the ballroom. "I've decided that we're going to hit the gallery while Carlo is still tied up in the reception line."

Nerves jumped in Natalie's stomach. "It's too soon. We just got here."

"Call it a preemptive strike. He won't expect anything this soon. And if the real diamond is in the gallery safe, we'll be gone before he's even suspicious."

The moment they reached the far door, he drew her through it and down across the hall.

"If you try to disable the camera, he'll send the troops after us," she said.

"Got it covered. Just follow my lead." With his hand on the knob, Chance paused long enough to meet her eyes. "Ready?"

Ready? How could she be when she had no idea what he was up to? But in spite of the nerves dancing in her stomach, Natalie felt the wave of excitement move through her. "Let's go for it."

"That's my girl," Chance said, leaning in to press his lips to hers as he opened the door and drew her into the small gallery. An instant later, he spun her around and pressed her against the closed door. Then his mouth was at her ear. "I'm going to tell you to strip for me. Make sure that you toss something to cover the camera."

Before she could reply or even think, his mouth was on hers again. For one giddy moment, she wondered if Stan was kissing Ollie or if Steven was kissing Calli. Then she no longer cared as the heat shot through her. His mouth was as ruthless and demanding as the hands he was running over her. As her knees turned to water and her arms moved around him, her body strained toward his. But there were too many clothes, too much padding in the way.

Suddenly, he backed away, swearing in frustration. "I can't feel you through all of those clothes. Get rid of them."

Natalie stared at him. His hair was mussed from her hands, and his eyes were hot with a mixture of desire and frustration. She felt an odd little thrill move through her. So he wanted her to strip? Okay, she'd strip.

Not moving, she said, "Sit down."

"I said I want your clothes off."

She took the feathered mask off first, then she moved toward him until her padded stomach was pressed against his. As she ran a finger down the front of his shirt to the waistband of his trousers, she said, "I'm going to take them all off. But it's going to take a while, so why not relax and enjoy it?" Then with her finger still prodding him, she urged him into the chair closest to the security camera.

The tie came first. She took her time pulling it off and then she looped it around his neck.

"What do you want me to take off next, Steven?" she asked as she backed a few steps away.

"The coat. Take the coat off."

She smiled as she freed the first button. "I can do that." Then she took her time, freeing one arm from the sleeve and then the other. Finally, as she lifted it and twirled it over her head, she considered. It was too soon to aim it at the camera. Besides, the security team might find the whole scenario more convincing if they could share a bit in the show. Natalie sent the coat flying wild. Then she fastened her gaze directly on Chance's eyes and smiled. "What would you like me to take off next, Sugar?"

He raised a hand and flicked a finger. "The trousers."

"Sure thing." Natalie unfastened the belt slowly. In spite of the nerves dancing in her stomach, she was finding it erotic to strip for Chance—and for whomever was watching through that camera.

So far, she hadn't exposed any skin, but she could feel the heat of Chance's gaze right through her clothes. In one long smooth movement, she pulled the belt free and set it on the floor next to her. A muscle twitched in his jaw. She made it twitch again as she sent the trousers pooling to the floor. "You like this, don't you?"

"Shoes."

The request surprised her. Maybe he was letting her know that he approved of her plan to prolong the striptease. She toed the shoes off, then crossed to him and placed one foot on his knee. Inch by inch, she rolled her socks down and pulled them off. She was close enough now that she could tell his breath wasn't steady. It grew more ragged as she repeated the process with the other sock. Then propping her hands on either side of the chair, she leaned in. Her mouth was a breath away from his when she said, "What next?"

He reached for her then, but she slipped away and laughed. "Let me choose this time. The shirt." She made it last—one button at a time, then the sleeves. She'd never before realized that stripping was as erotic and arousing for the stripper as it was for the audience. But just the brush of the fabric as she pulled it down her arms was sensitizing her skin. Raising the shirt high above her head, she twirled it just as she had the jacket. But this time, she aimed for the camera.

Bull's-eye.

"Take off that damn padding."

She did and she immediately bent over to take out her tools.

"Come here," Chance said. "I want to touch you now."

His voice was ragged, but when she glanced up, she saw that he wasn't in the chair anymore. Instead, he was opening the window. For their escape, she thought. Then she turned to the column and prayed that the safe was where she thought it was.

Though she hadn't heard him approach, he was there, lifting the bronze sundial off the wall. At the sight of the small safe, she let her heart take one little leap of triumph before she put on the earphones and began work.

"Here. This is where you like to be touched, isn't it?"

He wasn't touching her at all, but Natalie found she had to use all of her powers of concentration to keep from feeling that he was.

"And here. Right here where you're so wet and slick and hot."

Immediately, she was. She could feel the wetness pooling between her legs. Damn him. Promising herself that she was going to get even, she listened for the last tumbler to fall into place. The moment it did, she decided that two could play at the game that Chance had started.

In the huskiest voice she could muster, she said, "Bite me there. Yes. Oh yes. Yes." Then on a breathy moan, she opened the safe. The sight of the red velvet bag had her heart leaping.

Chance reached for it before she could, and a second later, the largest and most beautiful diamond she'd ever seen caught the light. To the naked eye, at least, it appeared to be real. But Chance was already examining it with a jeweler's loop. Without taking his eyes off of the diamond, he mouthed, "Keep the scenario going" and stepped up close to her.

She let out a long breathy moan. It wasn't hard, not with Chance's thigh pressing hard between her legs. "Yes. Oh, yes."

Only seconds ticked by, but to Natalie it seemed longer. Then Chance shook his head.

Swallowing her disappointment, she watched as he slipped the fake diamond back into the red velvet pouch and replaced it in the safe. As he rehung the bronze sun, she replaced her tools in the small pouch she wore. Then before she could even breathe, Chance had her pressed back against the column.

She didn't even have time to absorb the sensation before he rained a string of kisses along her cheek to her ear and whispered, "Before we leave, we have to play out this little scenario to the end. Otherwise, they'll wonder why suddenly everything got so quiet."

Then in a louder voice, he said, "I love to touch you here. And here." He ran his hands from her throat to her breasts and then slowly, lower and lower, until he slipped his finger beneath her panties and found her.

"And especially here." His mouth was so close that she could feel his breath on her lips. And he was barely touching her. His finger hardly entered her before withdrawing.

"I love to touch you here." His eyes were so focused, so hot. His fingers pushed into her—not far enough, not nearly—then withdrew.

She should push him away. In some far corner of her mind, she remembered that someone was listening to every word he said. And they still had to get the real diamond from the safe in Carlo's office. But with the pleasure streaming through her, she couldn't find the strength to raise her hands.

"Come for me, Calli. I want to see you come. Now."

Afterward, she would wonder if he could have made her come simply by commanding her to. There was something in his voice, something in the way he was looking at her...

But he didn't leave it to chance. As the heat of his words coursed through her, he slipped his fingers into her again—deeper this time. "Steven." That one gasp was all she managed before the orgasm that had been building since she'd started the strip tease slammed into her.

He held her there, propped against the column until the last wave of it receded, then he whispered against her ear. "Get dressed. We have to go now." She took some satisfaction in hearing that his voice wasn't quite steady.

She pulled on the clothes he handed her, a flood of emotions pouring through her. Shock, wonder—those were the only ones she could identify easily. And just below the surface, racing through her veins, was fear. No one had ever had this kind of effect on her, this kind of power over her. What was she going to do when their adventure was over?

"Ready?"

The whispered question had her dragging her thoughts back to the present. Chance was stooping at the open window, planting a listening device. If and when Carlo sent security to check the room, they'd have some advance warning.

At least that was the plan as he'd described it to her in the bathroom.

Chance crossed to the chair he'd been seated in and tucked a small tape recorder under it. For as long as the tape lasted, all anyone would hear would be a couple making love. The plan had been to play the tape from the moment she'd finished her striptease and blocked the camera. But Chance had decided to improvise.

There'd be time enough to worry about that after they'd finished what they came here to do. She moved to the window.

As he joined her, she became aware for the first time that he was wearing a cape and a mask.

On some level, she'd been aware that the clothes he'd handed her fit like a second skin, but it was only when he handed her a mask that she realized they were wearing new costumes. A quick glance down at her own confirmed her suspicion. Batman and Cat Woman.

Clever, she decided. The outfits would help them blend into the darkness of night and if they were caught, the new costumes should buy them a little time.

Chance said nothing as he threw one leg over the window ledge. His movements were smooth as he twisted and drew his other leg out. Then he was gone.

The only sound in the room came from the tape as she murmured Steven's name. Even above the scent of flowers from the garden, she caught the smell of sex. Anyone entering would have to be convinced that someone had made love in this room. Was that why Chance had made her come? Was it simply his way of being thorough? Or had it simply been to buy them extra time?

Later, she promised herself. Later, she'd not only have answers, she'd have revenge. Natalie threw one leg over the edge of the sill, twisted, wiggled and let gravity pull her until only her fingers were gripping the window ledge. Then she dropped.

The impact was still singing up her legs when Chance grabbed her hand and they began to edge their way along the wall of the house.

CARLO SCANNED the ballroom as he listened to the report from his chief of security through the small receiver in his ear. The shooter they'd been interrogating all day had finally named the man who'd hired him. Hassam Aldiri.

The news confirmed what Carlo had already suspected. Aldiri had a reputation for ruthlessness and Carlo had heard that the man would do anything to get what he wanted.

Lifting a hand, Carlo rubbed at the knot of tension that had settled at the back of his neck. Soon it would turn into the same raging headache he always got when he had to suppress his anger.

He was angry—furious—because Aldiri had hired someone to shoot a guest on his estate. And he was also angry at himself for not anticipating that a man with Aldiri's reputation might try something like this.

"Before you dispose of the shooter," Carlo said into his microphone, "I want to know how he got past my security system."

"Yes, sir."

Carlo let his gaze sweep the room again.

"And about the other matter, sir?"

A couple dressed as Oliver and Hardy had slipped into his gallery fifteen minutes ago and were currently making love. Carlo knew from an earlier report that the couple was Steven Bradford and Calli. Thanks to his security staff, he knew the identity of every person in the main salon.

He also knew about Calli's striptease. Evidently, Bradford and Calli weren't as upset by the shooting as he was. His gaze rested on Risa Manwaring and Armand Genovese. They'd arrived together as Napoleon and Josephine, and currently they were dancing.

As far as he knew, they'd met each other for the first time at dinner last night. Had they teamed up to buy the diamond? That would surely make tonight's auction more interesting...and profitable.

Carlo rubbed at the back of his neck again. Part of his tension was due to the fact that he still wasn't sure if one of his new guests was Chance Mitchell.

"Should I send someone into the gallery, sir?"

Carlo dragged his attention back to the voice in his ear. "You haven't lost the audio in the room?" he asked.

"No. They're getting that loud and clear."

Carlo bit back a smile. He could imagine that the volume was turned up high in the security room, and there must have been a loud groan of protest when they'd lost the video. For a moment, he debated whether or not to send guards into the gallery. Doing so might embarrass the couple, and they'd already been shot at today.

Glancing at his watch, he said, "I'll handle it in about fifteen minutes. But let me know if you lose the audio."

"Yes, sir."

Out of the corner of his eye, he saw Lisa approaching with Hassam Aldiri at her side. So the man had tried to kill the competition. On one level, Carlo could understand and admire that. He wouldn't forget that the attempt had been made on his estate, but for tonight, he'd concentrate on business.

Turning, he smiled as Aldiri reached him.

"Ms. McGill tells me that you will be auctioning the jewel tonight?" Hassam said.

Carlo glanced at his watch again. "In about two hours."

"I will top any offer that you receive," Aldiri said. "I want that diamond."

A man who didn't mince words, Carlo thought as he watched Aldiri move away. For the first time all evening, Carlo felt some of his tension ease. If the price went up high enough, perhaps he could forgive Aldiri for trying to shoot one of his guests. Turning to Lisa, he said, "It promises to be a profitable evening."

CHANCE MOVED as swiftly as he could along the wall of the villa. The clock was ticking. The tape he'd set in the gallery would last for ten minutes—if Carlo let it run to the end.

Flowering trees grew so close that now and again, he had to lift them away so that he and Natalie could squeeze by. Taking the path through the gardens would have been quicker, but he had no way of knowing how many security men were monitoring the cameras or how often the various sites rotated on the monitor screens. He wasn't taking the chance of letting one of those cameras pick up anything suspicious. The longer they kept their attention focused on the gallery, the better.

Just ahead, a palm tree butted up so close against the house that he ducked low and drew her around it. They had about one hundred yards left to go before they reached the courtyard near Carlo's office.

Natalie followed quietly behind him. She hadn't said a word since he'd touched her. He'd already asked himself what he'd been thinking. But he hadn't been thinking at all. Bringing her to orgasm certainly hadn't been part of the plan. They'd had a recording that they were going to play for the benefit of the men looking at the monitors. His job had been to place the listening device while she opened the safe. But the moment she'd started stripping, something had come over him.

She'd come over him. His mind should have been totally focused on the job. Instead, it had been focused on her. It was Natalie's tug on his hand that made him stop. When he turned, she whispered, "Here."

He glanced at the top of the wall and spotted the camera. It was aimed into the courtyard. If she hadn't spotted it, he wouldn't have stopped, and they'd have gone past Carlo's office and then wasted some of the precious moments they had by backtracking. Later, he promised himself. Later he would sort out what had happened to him in the gallery. Right now, he had a job to finish.

Pulling the tranquilizer gun out of the pouch he wore around his waist, he handed it to her. If they were lucky, the guard would be stationed on the patio. It would take less time to put him out of commission if they didn't have to lure him out of Carlo's office.

Leaning down, he cupped his hands. After she placed her foot in them, he gave her a moment.

"Ready," she whispered.

He straightened and boosted her up the wall.

NATALIE DUG her fingers into the crevices in the wall as she shifted first one foot and then the other onto Chance's shoulders. When she was sure she had her balance, she moved her hands to the top of the wall and slowly straightened until she could see over the edge. The patio was dim, illuminated only by the light spilling out from the office. But the French doors were open.

And then she spotted the glow of a cigarette. The guard was standing in the shade of a palm tree three feet to the left of the open door. She could hardly make him out, and she was only going to get one shot.

Heart hammering, she reached into her belt and pulled out the tranquilizer gun. Drawing in a deep breath, she aimed it in the direction of the palm tree. All she could see was the glow of the cigarette, and it wasn't moving. Impossible to tell if the guard was standing to the left or the right of that glowing circle of light. Was he sitting or standing?

She picked up a loose stone from the top of the wall and pushed it onto the patio. The guard moved toward the sand, stepping out from beneath the palm. Natalie aimed and fired.

"What the—"

She saw him raise a hand to his shoulder, then fall to the ground. Chance's hands gripped her ankles, lifting her until she could work the top half of her body over the wall. While Chance climbed up the wall to join her, she crawled over to the security camera and pointed it out at the gardens. If they were lucky, the guard watching the monitors wouldn't even realize that it had been shifted.

"Ready?" Chance asked.

Yes," she said as she began to lower her body over the edge of the wall. They dropped together.

Chance glanced at his watch. "The tape I left in the gallery just ran down," he said as they moved toward the French doors.

Natalie felt a rush of adrenaline. The clock was ticking now.

Moving quickly, she entered Carlo's office. The safe was just where she suspected—behind the painting at the back of his desk.

Her stomach sank. "I've never opened this kind of a safe before. Maybe, you should—"

"You can do it," Chance said.

She took one moment to gather her thoughts and then focused all her attention on the combination.

15

CARLO WAS MORE FURIOUS than he had ever been in his life. The headache raging behind his eyes only intensified when he walked into his gallery with Lisa and two security guards and saw the scattered clothes and the open window. After striding toward it, he glanced at the ground below.

"They're not here." He spoke into the microphone that connected him with his security chief. "Secure the grounds. No one is to leave this estate until they're found."

He turned to Lisa and the two security men who'd followed him into the room. "Check the Venetian room and see if they're there."

When Lisa didn't follow the guards, he said, "Go back to the salon. I need you there."

"What is going on?" she asked.

"I intend to find out. Go."

He followed her to the door and locked it behind her.

Then with a sliver of fear skipping up his spine, he went to the column and removed the bronze sundial. His fingers shook as he opened the safe. When he saw the red velvet pouch, his frown deepened. They hadn't broken into the safe. Otherwise, surely the diamond would be gone. Unless…had they had time to open the safe and discover that the diamond inside was a fake?

Clamping down tightly on his anger, Carlo focused as he surveyed the room again. They'd convinced his security staff that they'd come in here for sex. And the room smelled of it. So why had they exited through the window? Why not put their costumes back on and rejoin the party?

Or had they simply decided to take their lovemaking to a more private place?

Carlo studied the room. Clothes had been tossed everywhere. Trousers covered the security camera, one shirt hung over the back of a Louis XIV chair, another draped a Chinese vase a few feet from where he was standing. Next to it was the undergarment that had given Oliver Hardy his added girth.

Squatting down, Carlo turned the garment over. No padding. Whatever had been inside was something they'd taken with them. A new costume? Safecracking tools?

Had they come in here merely to throw him off and give themselves extra time to break into his office safe?

His gaze shifted to the window. Once they'd dropped into the garden, they'd only have to circle the house to reach the entrance to his private wing.

As Carlo strode toward the door, his mouth curved in an appreciative smile. Clever, he thought as he replayed in his mind every scene, every impression that he'd taken in since Steven Bradford and Calli had arrived on his estate. They were a couple who couldn't bear to be parted for very long, who couldn't keep their hands off one another. And they'd managed to create the illusion that there was more between them than sex.

No one, not his chief of security, and not even *he* had been overly suspicious when they'd sneaked into his gallery for a "quickie."

Oh, yes, they were much more clever than he'd anticipated. One of them must indeed be Chance Mitchell. It had been a long time since he'd had to pit himself against such a worthy opponent.

A new thought occurred to him. Could he be wrong about Aldiri? Had this "Chance" arranged for the shooting this morning just to throw him off? If so, he or she was very clever indeed. As he exited the room and relocked the door, Carlo spoke into the microphone that connected him to his chief of security. "Meet me at my office."

But Chance wasn't clever enough. The safe in his office wouldn't be as easy to open as the one in the gallery. It was a new model, and he'd had to practice on it for hours before he'd become sensitized to the fall of the tumblers.

IT'S TAKING TOO LONG. Natalie tried to ignore the nagging little voice in the back of her head as seconds ticked away. The muggy night air defeated the air-conditioning in the small room. She'd taken off her mask, and still she could feel sweat trickle down the back of her neck.

If her fingers slipped at this point… Very carefully, she lifted them from the lock and wiped them on her costume.

"Here," Chance whispered as he handed her a handkerchief.

"Thanks," she said. Where was Carlo right now, she wondered as she wiped her fingertips. He'd had plenty of time to go into his gallery, open his safe and see that the false diamond was still there. If the real diamond was here in his office suite, he'd check on it. He could be on his way.

The sound of static drifted in through the French doors, and her heart skipped a beat. Someone was trying to contact the guard she'd stunned. Time was running out.

She closed her fingers over the lock again. She had three parts of the combination. And she'd only had to try once for the last number. All she needed was for one more tumbler to slip into place. Just one more tiny click.

Chance said nothing, but she could feel him shift behind her so that his back was to hers. That way he could face both doors. Time was just about up.

She began to turn the lock very slowly. Seconds stretched into minutes, but she heard nothing. An icy sliver of fear slid up her spine, and she lifted her hand again. "I think I missed it. I must have missed it. I have the first three numbers. Maybe you'd better give it a try."

Chance placed a hand on her shoulder. "Start over if you have to. I fixed the lock so they'll have to force the door. There's still time."

But there wasn't. They both knew that. Natalie drew in a shaky breath and let it out. "I—"

Chance squeezed her shoulder. "You can do it, Nat."

Natalie went perfectly still. Later she would wonder whether it was Chance's belief in her that did it. Or perhaps it was his hand on her shoulder—that simple physical connection. Whatever it was, she could feel her self-doubt drain away as swiftly as if someone had pulled a plug. Suddenly, her mind was crystal-clear and her fingers felt each and every groove on the lock.

The same thing had happened the first time that she'd opened a safe. From the time she was little, her father had let her play with the one he'd kept in his office. She couldn't have been more than seven or eight the first time she'd cracked it.

Opening locks had been a game then, something she'd done in the precious time that her father had spent alone with her. With Rory he'd played cards. With Sierra he'd read books. But during the time he'd spent with her, they'd worked on locks. Even that first time, the last number had given her trouble. She recalled how he'd put a hand on her shoulder and said, "You can do it, Nat. Trust in your talents. You can do anything you want."

And she could. After drawing in a deep breath, she held it and focused all her attention on the connection between her mind and her fingers. The only sound in the room was the soft whir of the overhead fan. But even that faded when she felt the tiny click.

Someone pounded on the door.

With steady hands, she opened the door of the safe, grabbed the black velvet bag, and checked the contents. In it lay a diamond, the twin to the one they'd found in the gallery safe. There was no time for the

jeweler's loop this time. Chance barely had time to replace it with the fake diamond they'd brought with
them before the wood frame of the door began to splin-
ter.

Together they closed the safe and replaced the
painting.

The noise at the door grew louder, and wood splin-
tered again.

Chance grabbed her arm and pulled her toward the
French doors. Shouts came from beyond the patio
wall.

They were trapped. For one moment they stood
frozen in the frame of the open French doors. Shouts
beyond the patio were getting closer, louder. The door
to the office was about to give. Chance stripped off his
mask and threw it toward the patio wall. Then he
shoved her behind a floor-to-ceiling drape at the side
of the door. A second later, Natalie felt her breath go
out on a whoosh as he flattened her against the wall.
Heart hammering, she waited.

The door gave first and there was the sound of
guards rushing forward. Then the darkness fled as
someone flipped on the lights.

"Get out of the way."

Natalie recognized Carlo's voice even when he
slipped into Italian and swore viciously. He must have
seen the guard lying on the patio.

There was a rush of wind to her left as guards entered through the French doors. For one long second,
the drape covering them puffed out. Natalie could have
sworn that her heart skipped three beats until it settled
around them again.

"Tell me you've got them," Carlo said.

His voice was close now—inches away. Chance had gone still as a statue, but she could feel every muscle in his body tense.

"No, sir. There's no sign of them. All we got is this."

Carlo swore again. And again, the curtain shifted with the breeze. This time, out of the corner of her eye, Natalie caught a quick glimpse of Carlo standing in the doorway, taking something from the guard. If he turned right now, he would see them.

It came to her in a flash that Chance would be the one Carlo would catch sight of first. Chance would be the one that Carlo would shoot. She felt her heart stop and then the drape settled around them in slow motion.

"They can't be far. Cover the beach and the woods. I want them caught. Bring them to me alive, if possible."

In some part of her mind, Natalie knew that the guards had left and Carlo had moved away. The room had become silent except for the sound of the overhead fan whirring. Then she heard a scraping sound. Her heart skipped a beat. Carlo must be removing the painting so that he could check the safe.

Seconds ticked away. Natalie had to remind herself to breathe slowly, silently. What would happen if he discovered that the diamond in the pouch was a fake?

"Lisa?" Carlo had to be talking to Lisa on his cell phone.

"Everything is under control. I have the diamond right here in my hand. No. I don't have them yet. But I've issued orders that no one is allowed to leave the estate."

Chance shifted slightly. For one long moment, Natalie wondered if he would step from behind the curtain to confront his old enemy. The urge to do just that must be tearing him apart. She found his hand and gripped it tightly in hers.

"Tell Aldiri and the others that the auction will take place in an hour."

Carlo's voice was firm now, without a trace of the temper and anger that had filled it when he'd come into the room.

"You worry too much. I'm bringing the diamond with me. Tell them one hour from now in the gallery."

Natalie counted off ten beats as she listened to the sounds of Carlo closing the safe, replacing the painting and leaving the room. It was ten beats more before Chance stepped away from her and drew her from behind the drape.

She threw her arms around him then and held tight. A flood of emotions swept through her. He was safe. They both were for the moment, and she didn't want to let him go. Natalie wasn't sure how long they both stood like that before Chance drew away. "We have to go."

"I thought you were going to step out and confront him," she said.

Chance met her eyes steadily. "I was."

"But you didn't. Why not?"

"Because I knew my partner would follow right behind. Besides, I came up with a plan." He took a piece of paper from Carlo's desk and wrote one word. "Gianni."

Natalie understood exactly what he was doing. She thought of the young boy betrayed by his friend and sent to jail for something he hadn't done. Then she let herself imagine Carlo finding and reading that note—after the auction.

Meeting Chance's eyes, she said, "He thinks he still has the real diamond."

Chance smiled at her. "Ego. He didn't think that we could pull it off, and he found a diamond in each safe. So he didn't bother to check." He placed the note in the middle of Carlo's desk.

"And he won't find it until after the auction."

"Oh, I think the fake will be discovered before that," Chance said. "I can't imagine any of those prospective buyers parting with a cent until they authenticate the diamond."

"They won't be too happy with Carlo when they realize it's a fake," Natalie said. "And I don't think I'd want any of those characters unhappy with me."

"Hopefully, the fear of retribution will keep Carlo here on his estate until I can get Interpol to send someone to arrest him," Chance said.

She threw her arms around Chance and gave him a quick kiss. "I wish I'd known you when you were Gianni."

FOR A MOMENT, Chance said nothing. He simply looked at her. Her words and the simple gesture of affection unlocked something deep inside of him and released a flood of emotions. A thousand images flashed into his mind—a kaleidoscope of everything that had happened in the short time since they had begun this crazy adventure together.

She was the most amazing woman he'd ever

known. And the most complicated. There were so many facets to her. In the moonlight that poured into the room, he saw that her eyes were bright with excitement and triumph. He'd seen those eyes so many ways. Filled with a cool, steady courage. Lighted with laughter. And darkened by passion.

And he'd seen the intensity in those eyes when she was thinking only of him, feeling only him. He wanted to tell her. He needed to—

A crack split the still night air, and Chance dragged his thoughts back to the present. "C'mon."

"Was that gunfire?" Natalie asked as they raced into the courtyard.

"Tracker's version of misdirection. One of his men is presently escaping in the inflatable boat we were supposed to use."

"Supposed to use?" Natalie asked.

Chance leaned down, scooped up the guard's weapon, and tossed it to her. "That's one of the reasons I don't have much use for plans. They usually have to be changed."

To what? But Natalie didn't ask the question as she stuffed the gun into her waistband. Chance had already moved to the wall and was cupping his hands. By the time he'd boosted her to the top and joined her, they could hear running footsteps beyond the trees that grew along the wall and farther away came the rapid cough of automatic fire.

Together, they dropped to the ground.

"Where to?" Natalie asked. But Chance was already drawing her in the opposite direction from which they'd come. As they edged their way between the trees and the wall of the villa, Natalie realized one amazing thing. She was almost getting used to Chance's habit of improvising plans on the spur of the moment. Almost, she reminded herself when she realized they'd made a complete circle of the villa. By the time they reached the iron gate that closed off the kitchen wing, she could hear the music from the ballroom once more.

Then Chance stopped and drew out the cell phone he always used to communicate with Tracker. Holding it to his ear, he said one word, "Now."

A few moments later, the iron gate to the kitchen wing swung open and a white van moved forward. Natalie barely had time to read the words, "At Your Service," on the paneling before a large woman in a tight-fitting white uniform climbed out and said in a husky voice, "Catering to your every need."

Natalie was reaching for the gun at her waist when Chance grabbed her wrist. "It's Tracker. C'mon."

He drew her with him as the "woman" opened the back doors to the van. Natalie had a hard time recognizing Tracker McBride. He was wearing a blond wig, and unless she'd known, she wouldn't have guessed that the snug-fitting uniform hid the tough, athletic body that she knew he possessed.

"The security is tight here. The guard searched the back of the van when I came in because I wasn't on his list from the catering company."

"Do I want to know how you convinced him to let you in?" Chance asked, amusement clear in his voice as he climbed into the back of the van and held out a hand to Natalie.

Tracker patted the blond wig he was wearing and wiggled his hips. "My charm, of course. We developed quite a rapport."

"It'll be tougher this time," Chance warned. "Carlo has instructed the guards that no one is allowed to leave."

"I love a challenge," Tracker said with a grin before he shut the doors.

"He seems confident," Natalie murmured.

"If anyone can get us out, he can," Chance assured her.

"He'll want to search the van." Tracker spoke from behind the wheel at the front of the van this time. "Think you can handle it?"

"No problem," Chance said. "I've got my partner with me."

Partner. The sound of the word warmed Natalie and eased the jumping nerves in her stomach. Neither she nor Chance spoke as the van moved forward and eventually pulled to a stop at the gate.

"Lots of excitement," Tracker said to the guard, using his husky almost falsetto voice.

"Mr. Brancotti is a stickler when it comes to security, and there was a problem earlier today. I can't let anyone leave."

Tracker laughed. "Do I look like I pose any threat to Mr. Brancotti? And you checked me out earlier."

There was a pause, and Natalie wondered just what Tracker was up to.

"Be a sport," Tracker continued. "I've delivered the extra food they needed, and I have a date tonight. You can check the back of the van."

There was another silence, but Natalie could hear the guard and Tracker walking along the side of the van. It was dark and she could barely see Chance, but they moved in unison, flattening themselves into the corners on either side of the doors.

A moment later the doors opened and the guard, flashlight in one hand and gun in the other, stepped up into the van. Natalie slipped her foot out, and when he stumbled, Chance clipped him hard on the back of his neck. The man fell like a stone.

"Nice going," Tracker said as Chance leaned down to tie the guard's hands behind his back. "You guys make a great team."

Natalie turned to Tracker. "How did you convince him to take a look?"

Tracker shot her a grin. "Money. Sometimes, it works a lot faster than my charm—" he smoothed his hands over his hips "—though I can't imagine why."

NATALIE DRIFTED awake as if she were surfacing from a long dive. The scent of coffee was the first thing that her conscious mind identified. Then everything came back to her in a rush. She and Chance had stolen the Ferrante diamond from Carlo Brancotti, and they'd left a fake one behind. Mission accomplished!

Once they'd taken care of the guard at the gate, their escape with Tracker in the van had gone without a hitch. Carlo's security team had been focused on the beach area. For a moment, she allowed her mind to linger on those few charged moments in the van when she and Chance had been so in tune about how to take out the guard. They might have been working together for years.

The events after that had been less clear. At some point after they'd boarded Steven Bradford's plane, the adrenaline rush she'd been riding on all day had faded, and she'd fallen asleep. She vaguely remembered that Chance had carried her into the bedroom. Then nothing.

Opening her eyes, she saw that she was still in the bedroom on the plane. And Chance was gone. But he'd been here. At some point, she'd felt him lying beside her, holding her. The pillow next to hers still bore the indentation from his head. As she ran her hand over it, she realized that the plane was stopped.

Just when had they landed? Throwing the covers off, she noted that she was still wearing her Cat Woman costume. She checked the bathroom first, but it too was empty. After taking a moment to brush her teeth and run her fingers through her hair, she moved quickly to the door.

But it was Tracker and not Chance that she saw sitting at a table, tapping at the keys of his laptop. He glanced up immediately. "Good morning. Want some coffee?"

"Where's Chance?" A funny little feeling had settled in the pit of her stomach the moment she'd seen that the airplane door stood open.

Tracker handed her a mug of steaming coffee. "I was under orders to let you sleep."

"Where's Chance?" Natalie repeated.

Tracker shot her a smile. "Promise not to kill the messenger?"

At any other time, she might have been charmed. Hell, she might even have been amused. But the funny little feeling was making her stomach roll and her throat tighten. "He's gone, isn't he?"

Tracker sighed. "Yeah. I told him he should wake you, but he had to get the diamond back to the London office. He tried to get out of it, but there's some red tape he has to take care of in person."

In some part of her mind, Natalie listened to Tracker's explanation. It was logical, perfectly understandable. Chance's part of the job wasn't over. So he'd had to fly off to London to tie up loose ends. A sickening sense of déjà vu filled her.

"Chance has to move quickly," Tracker said. "He hoped you'd understand."

Natalie thought she understood very well. The adventure was over, and a man like Chance—a man so like her father—would want to be on to the next one as soon as possible.

"Yes," she said. She did understand. She'd signed on for the job, and now it was over. She felt the prick of tears behind her eyes, and she blinked—but it was too late. The first drop slid down her cheek.

"Shit," Tracker said as he pushed the laptop away and rose. "Natalie, don't." He drew her against him and held her. "I told him to wake you and explain it himself. But he—"

Natalie held herself stiff. She had to stop crying. There was no sense to it. She never cried. She hadn't, not once, since her father had left.

"He's coming back, Natalie. He told me to tell you—"

Tracker broke off when suddenly she used all of her strength to push away.

"What is it?" he asked.

She scrubbed tears away with the heel of her hand. "You called me Natalie."

For a second a puzzled expression crossed his face. "Yes…oh, shit. Shit. Shit."

"If you know I'm not Rachel Cade, then—" As Tracker continued to swear, Natalie remembered the moment when she'd been trying to hear the last part of the combination to Carlo's safe. Chance had used her father's exact words. "You can do it, Nat."

He'd called her Nat. The sharp band of pain tightening around her heart had her rubbing her chest with her fist.

"He's known all along, hasn't he? That I'm Natalie, not Rachel Cade?"

"He…I…." It was pure panic that she saw on Tracker's face now. Later, much later, she was going to remember that with some amusement. She promised herself that. But right now, there were too many other emotions spiking through her. One of them was anger, the cold, icy kind. That was the one she latched on to.

He'd known who she was from the beginning. And he'd played along with her because he liked the game. It had all been a game.

"He wanted to stay and explain—"

Holding up a hand, she said, "Enough. You don't have to explain. I get it." Then she held out her hand palm up. "Since I had to leave the Brancotti estate without packing, I'll require cab fare to my apartment."

16

"Ooh, Detective Natalie! Your hair! What have you done?"

The moment Rad had caught sight of her, he'd clapped two palms to his cheeks and stared. Now the majority of the people waiting for a table at the Blue Pepper was staring at her too.

"You've cut it." Rad pressed the back of one hand against his forehead and the palm of the other over his heart. "You've *cut* your lovely hair!"

"Yes, I've cut my hair." Natalie fluffed the ends with one hand. The color was back to normal. And so was she. That's what she'd kept telling herself during the week she'd been back.

"It will grow in." Rad spoke in the hushed tone of voice one might use to express sympathy at a wake.

Because she was pretty sure he was comforting himself and not her, Natalie found herself biting back a grin. "Hair has a tendency to do that." Maybe her sisters had been right to insist that they get together for dinner. "Are my sisters here?"

"Sure thing." Rad's face brightened. "I gave them a table on the patio. They're already enjoying the appetizer sampler."

Natalie drew in a steadying breath as she followed Rad through the crowd and down the three steps. Being on the patio was a good thing. Better to face all your ghosts. Better to— Her heart nearly stopped as she stepped onto the dance floor. The salsa band was playing the same tune that she and Chance had danced to on the night that she'd taken him up on his first proposition.

Memories of that night and others streamed into her mind—the way he'd touched her, held her, filled her. The memories and the sensations hadn't dimmed any more than the ache in her heart had.

But they would, she told herself firmly. And maybe she wouldn't let her hair grow in. Maybe she could never be the same Natalie Gibbs she'd been before Chance Mitchell. So what?

Lifting her chin, she followed Rad off the dance floor.

"Here she is," Rad announced as they reached the table.

Any confidence Natalie might have built up faded the moment she looked at her sisters. She could tell by the expression on their faces that she wasn't quite back to the old Natalie Gibbs yet. In fact, what she saw in their eyes was what she'd been denying every time she let herself look in the mirror.

Rory had frozen in place with a stuffed mushroom halfway to her mouth. Rory never let anything interfere with her appetite.

Sierra had her hands clasped tightly together in front of her, the way she always did when she was really nervous or worried.

Hell. Natalie knew she looked like shit.

"Her lovely hair will grow back," Rad said.

When silence continued to stretch at the table, Rad cleared his throat and said, "Well. How about I bring the drink of the week—a frozen pineapple margarita?"

Rory cut him off by raising her free hand. "Three very dry martinis with olives. And keep them coming."

"Excellent choice," Rad said as he hurried away.

Sierra took Natalie's hand. "What happened to you?"

Natalie found she had to speak around a lump in her throat. "I'm fine."

Rory set her stuffed mushroom down. "You have black circles the size of Wyoming around your eyes."

"I've been working."

"And not sleeping," Sierra said. "Or eating. Tell us."

Natalie sighed. A triplet could never have secrets. Finally, she said, "Sometimes when you risk everything for something, you don't get it."

And then she told them the whole story.

"THIS ISN'T MY HOTEL," Chance said as Tracker eased the car to the curb in front of the Blue Pepper.

"We thought we'd have a drink first," Tracker said. "Lucas is buying."

Searching his mind for an excuse to bow out, Chance stepped onto the curb. Above the traffic noises on the street came the faint sounds of laughter and music from the patio. He recognized the song the band was playing. It was the same one that he'd danced to with Natalie three months ago. That's when everything had started between them. No, he corrected himself as nervousness twisted in his stomach. Everything had started between them the first moment he'd seen her. Had that been when he'd fallen in love with her?

Panic slithered in to join the nervousness. "You guys go ahead," he said. "I've got some business to take care of." Truth was he had a plan to make. And he was lousy at them. "I'll just take a cab—"

Tracker gripped one arm and Lucas the other. "Sophie's holding our table."

"And Mac will be very annoyed if we don't bring you," Lucas added. "Besides you owe us. I provided my boat and my chief of security for this little Florida caper of yours."

"Yeah," Tracker put in. "And don't forget the effort I put into saving your sorry ass. My arches are still sore from those high heels I had to wear. The very least you owe us is a drink and the rest of the story."

Chance sighed and let himself be led into the Blue Pepper. It was the last place he wanted to be. Memories of Natalie were already flooding his mind. The past week had been hectic, tying up the Ferrante diamond case in London and seeing to it that "Carlo Brancotti" was finally behind bars. Now, he needed a cool head to think.

"Ah, Mr. Wainwright. Welcome, welcome, welcome."

At first, Chance couldn't see who was speaking, but on the last "welcome," a short man with spikey red hair burst through the throng of people waiting for tables.

"Hi, Rad," Lucas said. "Is my wife here?"

"She's with Miss Sophie. This way," the man said as he waved a hand and led them up the stairs and into the bar.

At least they weren't going to have to sit on the patio, Chance thought. After greeting and being hugged by Sophie and Mac, he found himself wedged between the two women in the corner of a circular banquette.

Sophie poured a glass of beer from the pitcher in the center of the table and handed it to him. Then Tracker cleared his throat. "There's something you ought to know."

Something in the tone of his friend's voice had his stomach muscles clenching. "What?" He glanced around the table, noted the solemn expressions and fear streamed through him. "Has something happened to Natalie?"

"No." Mac spoke as Sophie laid a hand on Chance's arm. "She's fine. She's on the patio right now with her sisters."

Chance felt his throat go dry. "She's here." He wasn't ready to see her, and for the first time in his life he didn't trust himself to improvise. "I—"

Suddenly, he didn't care whether or not he had a plan. He had to see her. Hold her. Maybe the plan would come to him then.

"Let me out." He nudged Mac. "I need to see her."

"There's something you should know before you see her," Tracker said. "I—she knows you were aware all along that she was Natalie—that you were never fooled by the Rachel Cade disguise."

"You told her?" Chance asked.

"Hell, I didn't mean to. I slipped and called her Natalie."

Chance took a long swallow of the beer. "I take it she wasn't pleased."

"She wouldn't even let me drive her to her apartment," Tracker said.

"You don't have to lecture him," Sophie said before Chance could speak. "I already have. But you should have told her yourself."

"Before you took her to Florida with you," Mac added, then shook her head. "Pretending to believe that she was this Rachel Cade when all the time you knew she was Natalie…what were you thinking?"

Chance raised a hand, warding off their criticism. "I wasn't. But at the time, I—" At the time he'd been afraid she wouldn't come, and he'd wanted her with him. "I wasn't thinking clearly."

The two women exchanged glances, then Sophie spoke. "Tracker says you're nuts about her."

Chance pinned his friend with a look.

"Hey," Tracker said with a shrug. "I only calls 'em as I sees 'em."

"Don't look at me," Lucas said. "My advice is to plead the Fifth."

Chance glanced back at the two women. "Works for me."

Then to his surprise Mac and Sophie smiled at him.

"Since you are clearly nuts about her, we've decided to help you dig yourself out of the hole you're in," Sophie said.

Mac slid out of the banquette. "Go. Talk to her."

Chance felt his stomach plummet as he followed

Mac out of the banquette. Natalie was here. His intention had been to spend the night working out a strategy for what he knew he wanted to do. Maybe he'd call her in the morning. Or send her flowers and then drop in on her at work. Or…

Hell, it was the one time in his life that he dearly needed a plan, and he had no choice but to play it by ear.

"WELL, WHAT ARE YOU going to do about it?" Rory asked as she swirled her olive around in her drink and then popped it into her mouth.

"Do?" Natalie asked.

"Yes." Sierra reach over to pat her hand. "You always have a plan."

Natalie took a sip of her martini, then studied her two sisters over the rim of the glass. She'd just told them everything that had happened since she'd left Sophie's party with Chance, and they were looking a lot less worried than they'd been when she first sat down at the table.

"Right," Rory said around a mouthful of stuffed mushroom. "It sounds like you had a wonderful adventure down in Florida. But you're going to have to do something about Chance."

"No." Natalie shook her head. "I've had my adventure and I've had my fling. My plan is to go back to being Natalie Gibbs. Period."

"You're crazy about him," Sierra said in her quiet, certain voice.

"I'm…" The *not* stuck in her throat. Because Sierra was right. No one else in the world had ever made her feel the way Chance Mitchell had. She was very much afraid that she was in love with him. "I'm a mess," she finally admitted.

"Have one of these shrimp." Rory shoved the plate toward her.

Natalie shook her head, but she did take another sip of her drink. "He's walked out on me twice now."

"Yes, he has," Sierra said.

"The jerk," Rory said.

"I'll drink to that," Natalie murmured and did. For the first time since she'd walked off the plane a week ago, she didn't feel quite so numb. Perhaps it was the martini. Or maybe it was the little flame of anger that had flickered to life inside of her.

"He doesn't know who he's dealing with," Sierra said.

"No," Natalie agreed. He didn't.

"You've always been the one with courage. Harry was right when he called you his warrior. I've never once known you to walk away from anything," Sierra added.

Natalie's eyes narrowed. "You're trying that psychology stuff on me."

"She's trying the truth," Rory said.

"The way I see it, it all boils down to one question—do you want this man?" Sierra asked.

Natalie thought of all that had happened between them down in Florida. It hadn't just been about great sex. Finally, Natalie drew in a deep breath. "Yes, I want him."

"Then take a risk," Sierra said.

"And use your talents," Rory added.

Natalie glanced at her watch. Technically, she was

still on vacation. So there wouldn't be any trouble getting a few days off. Either Tracker or Lucas Wainwright should know where Chance could be contacted in London. And while she was finding out that information, she'd have time to plan.

"I've got to go," she said as she rose from her chair.

"Speak of the devil," Rory said.

Natalie felt the prickle of awareness at the same moment Rory spoke the words. Then turning, she felt that quick leap of her heart that only Chance could cause.

He was moving quickly through the crowd on the stairs. How long had he been in town? How had he known she was here?

The moment that his eyes met hers, she felt it right down to her toes. *I'm not ready for this.* That was the one solid thought that managed to tumble into her mind as she walked to meet him in the center of the dance floor. Couples moved around them. Natalie could see that he looked tired—as if he hadn't slept in a week. That made her feel just a little bit better.

For a moment, neither of them spoke.

Then Chance said, "Natalie," and reached for her.

She took a quick step backward and folded her arms in front of her chest. "Why? Why didn't you tell me that you knew I wasn't Rachel Cade?"

He frowned. "Don't you think I asked myself that a hundred times? I should have. I know that. But once we were down in Florida, I told myself that it would be safer if I didn't."

"Safer?" Her brows shot up and she began to tap her foot.

"Okay. I didn't tell you because I was afraid at first

that you wouldn't come with me and, later, that you wouldn't stay."

"So it was the job all along."

"No."

She saw the anger flash into his eyes, felt it in the way he grabbed her arms. But she planted two hands on his chest and held her ground.

"You were the one who masqueraded as Rachel Cade. Why did you put on the damn disguise in the first place?"

She lifted her chin. "Because you walked away from Natalie Gibbs."

"I didn't. I had a job."

She poked a finger into his chest. "You didn't leave a note. You didn't call for three months."

He held up his hands, palms out. "Okay. I plead insanity. But I'm not walking away this time."

In a move so quick that she couldn't prevent it, Chance pulled her onto her toes and kissed her.

As his taste, his heat, streamed through her, Natalie felt as if she were coming home. It would have been so easy to sink into that feeling, into him. But not yet. She hooked a foot around his ankle and gave him one good shove that sent him to the floor.

Couples scattered, and she heard a burst of applause. Out of the corner of her eye, she saw Tracker and Sophie on the side of the dance floor. Mac and Lucas stood behind them grinning.

"You go, girl!" Rory shouted.

"Trust in your talents," Sierra called, the laughter clear in her voice.

Natalie kept her eyes on Chance as he shot her a grin. It nearly melted her, but she wasn't through with him. Not yet. Planting her hands on her hips, she said, "You're a jerk."

"Okay. I plead guilty to that one."

There was another burst of applause from the crowd.

Chance held out his hand. "Help me up?"

Her brows shot up again. "Do I look like I have the word *Sucker* written on my forehead?"

CHANCE THREW BACK his head and laughed. This was his Natalie all right. He got up off the floor and faced her. "God, I've missed you. I liked Rachel. I've always had this thing for blondes."

"Really?" Her foot began to tap again.

Chance began to warm to his theme. "And Calli was really sexy. I had a real thing going for her."

"Yeah. I got that feeling."

She was softening. He was almost sure that he'd seen her lips twitch.

"But I missed you."

He waited a beat, and when she said nothing, he decided for the first time in his life to risk everything. "I have another proposition for you."

Her eyes narrowed and her foot tapped faster. "If you think—"

He raised a hand to stop her. "I thought we might go behind those potted trees over there—for old times' sake?"

"Forget it."

Oh, his Nat was back all right. He might have even begun to enjoy himself, if it weren't for the fear that had tied itself into a tight knot in his stomach. If he blew this— No, he wasn't going to blow it. He couldn't.

"Okay. I'll do it right here." He pulled the small box out of his pocket. Then he got to his knees and opened it.

"A ring? You brought me a ring?"

There was such astonishment on her face, in her voice, that a quick sliver of panic raced up his spine. Was he pushing her too fast? "Yeah. It doesn't have to be an engagement ring. It could just be a—"

Words slipped away as she dropped to her knees in front of him.

"Looks like an engagement ring to me," she said, meeting his eyes. "But if you're having second thoughts…"

"No." Chance met her eyes steadily and saw what he needed to see. "No second thoughts. How about you?"

She gave him a shaky smile. "Just about a thousand or so. I didn't plan on this." She drew in a breath and let it out.

He smiled at her. "Me either. But I'm good at improvising. So are you."

She looked down at the ring again. It was a big step, a huge one. And there wasn't a plan in the world that she could come up with to deal with it. But as Chance put his hands on her shoulders, she thought she could hear a voice telling her, "You can do it, Nat."

And then she heard Chance's voice. "I love you, Nat."

She met his eyes then and smiled. "I love you, too. So I guess we'll just have to make it up as we go along."

He kissed her then, and though she vaguely thought applause and shouts had broken out around them, the one thing that she was sure of was Chance.

Natalie's found her happy ending.
Now it's Rory's turn.
Don't miss the fireworks in
Blaze #188
THE DARE
by Cara Summers
June 2005
Here's a peek...

1

THIS WAS DEFINITELY her lucky day! Rory Gibbs barely kept herself from dancing a little jig. One of the two men at the registration desk had to be Jared Slade. She was sure of it. But which one? Taking two quick steps to her right, she ducked behind a potted palm tree and peered through the branches.

Was it the handsome, preppy looking blond? Or was it the shorter, tougher looking dark haired man who stood next to him?

Nerves simmering, Rory blew out a small bubble, then used her teeth and tongue to draw the gum back into her mouth. The dark haired man had given the name Jared Slade to the reception clerk, but the blond was the one signing the registration form. Rory was betting on the blond.

Maybe it was the shorter, darker one wearing horned-rimmed glasses, even though he looked more like an accountant than a man who ran a company. Rory blew another bubble.

The way she'd pictured him in her mind, Jared Slade had been larger and drop dead gorgeous. And in spite of the almost picture perfect good looks, he had an aura of danger about him. In fact, he'd looked quite a bit like her fantasy man.

Neither of the two men standing at the desk looked particularly dangerous. Rory licked another bubble off her lips. If there was one thing that twenty-six years and five career changes had taught her, it was the huge chasm that existed between fantasy and reality. The studious looking accountant was probably the real Jared Slade.

As she dug in her bag for her camera, she took a quick glance around the lobby. A third man had come through the revolving doors with Jared Slade. She'd been too intent on watching the other two at the desk to pay him much heed, but she did so now. He was a large man with dark hair, wearing black jeans, a leather jacket and dark glasses. He definitely had fantasy man possibilities.

Later, she would recall that she'd had time for that one quick thought before he lifted the dark glasses and shot a quick look in her direction. She felt her heart skip a beat and her mouth go dry. Then as those dark eyes locked on hers, she felt a little punch of something hot right in her gut and her mind went blank for a moment.

It was only when he turned back to talk to the bell captain that Rory remembered to breathe. And it was only as she drew in a second breath that the oxygen reached her brain and she began to think again.

Well. She'd never reacted that way to any other man. But then, this one was so much like the fantasy man she'd created in her head—tall, dark, and handsome in a rough edged sort of way. She began to chew on her bubble gum again.

Time for a reality check, she reminded herself. Mr.

Danger was probably a bodyguard with valet duties, since he seemed to be sorting out the luggage with the bell captain. When he glanced over in the direction of the registration desk, Rory scrunched herself farther down behind the palm tree. The last thing she needed was a run in with Jared Slade's bodyguard.

She should have worn something green, camouflage fatigues. For one long moment—even through the palm fronds—Rory felt the large man's eyes on her again. It felt like a mild sort of electrical shock along her nerve endings. She averted her own gaze and willed herself invisible. Her red boots would be hidden, but not the red cap. Her sisters constantly teased her about being a slave to fashion. Was she about to pay the price?

HUNTER MARKS FROWNED as he watched the woman in the red hat and boots squat down behind a tall potted palm. Who was she and what in hell was she doing? His eyes had been drawn to her from the moment he'd walked into Les Printemps. One glance had him thinking of pixies and elves. And that was not the usual turn his mind took when he looked at a woman. He prided himself on being practical rather than fanciful when it came to the female of the species.

This particular specimen had been seated on one of the settees, not sipping tea or a cocktail as the other occupants of the lobby were. Instead, she'd been scanning the crowd while she blew a huge bubble. When the bubble burst, he'd watched in amusement as she pulled it off her cheeks and nose and poked it back into her mouth.

He'd taken the time to study her face then. The cherry red lips had drawn his attention first, and he'd found himself wondering if they would carry the flavor of the bubble gum. The errant thought along with the tightening and hardening of his body surprised him.

Women never surprised him. And the pixie with the bubble gum was a far right turn from the type he usually dated. For starters, she looked too young. Of course the slight build could account for that—along with the hair. From what he could see of it—a few wisps that peeked out from beneath the red cap, she wore her dark hair shorter than most men. He shifted his gaze down the black jean jacket and jeans to the red boots and felt his body go even harder.

Then she glanced his way and for one long moment his gaze held hers. He felt a punch of desire so strong that for a moment he couldn't breathe. Then he felt his mind empty and fill again with images of her and what he'd like to do to her.

"Here you go, sir."

With some effort, Hunter dragged his mind back to reality as the bell captain handed him three tickets. His reaction to this woman was unprecedented.

"The briefcase and the laptop will be taken up to the Presidential Suite for Mr. Slade," the man said. "I'll handle it personally. And the suitcases will be up shortly."

"Appreciate it," Hunter said as he slipped a folded bill across the narrow counter. Then he leaned closer to the bell captain. "Do you see that woman over there—the one behind the palm tree?"

The bell captain took a moment to casually scan the lobby. Les Printemps was a small hotel that prided itself on calling each guest by name. Hunter had researched it himself. The management catered to a very select clientele, a mix of foreign diplomats and celebrities, who paid premium prices because they valued their privacy and expected the hotel to protect it at all costs.

"That's Miss Rory Gibbs, sir," the ball captain said, a wide grin spreading across his face.

"Is she staying here?" Hunter asked.

"No."

Hunter frowned. "I thought only registered guests were allowed in the lobby."

"She's meeting her fiancé here. She said her father brought her here for high tea once, and she wanted to relive the moment with her husband to be. Sweet little thing. She reminds me a bit of my daughter."

Hunter returned his gaze to Rory Gibbs just as she pulled a camera out of her purse.

Shit, he said to himself as he strode toward her. He prided himself on having a sixth sense where reporters were concerned. But this one had fooled him.

There were only three people in his organization who'd known he was checking into Les Printemps. And Ms Rory Gibbs was his ticket to finding out just who the traitor was in his organization.

Rory's heart was beating so fast that she was sure the two men at the reception desk could hear it. One at a time, she wiped her damp hands on her jeans. She couldn't afford to drop the camera. Dammit. She could still feel Jared Slade's bodyguard/valet watching her and he was having the oddest effect on her whole system.

Focus, she told herself. No one had ever taken a picture of Jared Slade, and no one had interviewed him. She intended to do both.

"We want you to enjoy your stay at Les Printemps, Mr. Slade," the neatly groomed woman behind the desk said as she pushed a key across the counter.

Rory noted that the dark-haired man picked it up. But it was the blond man who said, "Thank you."

They would turn around any minute and she would finally be looking at *Jared Slade*. Which one would he be?

Turn. Rory concentrated on sending out the message telepathically. But the blond was asking about the health club facilities. Jared Slade was known to be a health nut.

So the blond was Jared.

"Where's the best place to take a run?" the dark-haired man asked.

Or maybe the runner was Jared. And still they didn't turn around. So much for her telepathic powers.

Raising the camera, she pressed the button on the zoom lens and found herself viewing a close up of a palm leaf. She pushed it out of her way, only to discover that the two were moving away from the desk. She could see their faces in profile now. The darker-haired man was tough looking and built like a boxer. The blond had the long, rangy body of a swimmer.

If she'd had to bet money, she still would have placed it on the blond. But this was too important to merely trust in her luck. An exclusive interview with Jared Slade was her ticket to a permanent job on the staff of *Celebs* magazine. So she had to be sure. And she needed a picture for her editor. Edging her way out from behind the palm tree, she aimed the camera and said, "Jared Slade?"

The blond man turned first, and she had three quick shots of him before someone behind her said, "Stop right there."

Whirling, she saw the fantasy man—Mr. Danger—striding toward her. He looked every inch the body-guard now. In fact, the combination of sunglasses, black leather jacket and black jeans had her thinking for one giddy moment of the Terminator. Rory froze.

Later, she would wonder if it was the sheer size of the man that intimidated her for a moment. Or perhaps it was the odd little punch to her system again. The only thing she was certain of was that all of his atten-tion was totally focused on her. She could feel his pur-pose, feel *him* in every pore of her body. He was the Terminator personified.

When he was still a few yards away, he held out his hand. "I'll take that camera."

She clutched it close to her chest and debated for one more minute. Gibbs girls never ran. Her father had drummed that into her from the time she was a tod-dler. On the other hand, the Terminator was a lot big-ger than she was, and she wasn't about to give up her picture of Jared Slade. When he'd nearly reached her, she feinted to the right, then darted behind the palm tree. Once she'd cleared the branches, she raced for the lobby door.

HUNTER SWORE under his breath. By the time he skirted the damn potted palm, the little pixie had pushed her way through the front door.

"Stay here," he called over his shoulder to the two men who'd been at the registration desk. Then he ran toward the hotel entrance and made it out to the street just in time to see her turn the corner. By the time he reached it, she was nowhere in sight. She couldn't have reached the next corner, so she had to be in one of the shops.

Deliberately, he slowed his pace, allowing the other pedestrians on the street to flow past him. The first shop he passed had designer chocolates in the window. A quick glance inside told him that his quarry wasn't there, and there was no obvious place to hide. The second shop had lingerie displayed in the window, and he spotted her moving quickly toward the back of the store with an armful of lace and satin in tow.

Hunter glanced up at the name over the shop door and smiled slowly. This was his lucky day. Silken Fantasies was the very shop he'd come to DC to buy. It's location in the same block as Les Printemps was one of the reasons why he'd decided to stay at the small hotel. A quick glance at the tall, strikingly attractive woman behind the counter confirmed that she was the owner. At fifty, Irene Malinowitz was looking to retire so that she could play with her grandchildren. And Slade Enterprises was looking to turn Silken Fantasies into a very profitable chain.

Slowly Hunter backed out of the flow of traffic. He had to hand it to Rory Gibbs. She had a good plan. All she had to do was hang out in one of the dressing rooms until whoever was chasing her gave up.

Except he'd never given up in his life—even before

the time that he'd become Jared Slade. Added to that, she'd had the bad luck to run into a shop where he knew the owner. When she'd disappeared into one of the dressing rooms at the back of the shop, he moved closer to the window and considered his options. He wanted to talk to Miss Rory Gibbs. He also wanted that camera, he reminded himself. The best way to convince her that she'd taken a picture of the real Jared Slade would be to destroy the film.

Then he would ask her how she'd known that Jared Slade was going to be checking into Les Printemps. Very few people in his organization had known that. Denise Martin, his chief administrative assistant in his Dallas office and the two men he was traveling with— Michael Banks, his executive assistant, and Alex Santos, his accountant. Up until now, he'd trusted all three of them.

But for the last three months, someone had been causing problems for his company. There'd been an episode of stomach poisoning in his hotel in Atlanta and a fire that had caused some damage in a factory in upstate New York. He'd flown in to deal with each crisis personally. And both times he'd received a note—*No matter what you do, soon the world will know who you are and what you've done.*

Someone was threatening to reveal who he used to be, and Ms. Rory Gibbs might very well know who the writer of those notes was.

Taking his cell phone out, Hunter pressed in numbers. Little did she know it, but Ms. Rory Gibbs had just walked into a trap.

If you enjoyed what you just read,
then we've got an offer you can't resist!

Take 2 bestselling love stories FREE!

Plus get a FREE surprise gift!

Coming in June 2005
from Silhouette Desire

DYNASTIES: THE ASHTONS

*A family built on lies…brought together
by dark, passionate secrets.*

Sara Orwig's
ESTATE AFFAIR
(Silhouette Desire #1657)

Eli Ashton couldn't resist one night of passion
with Lara Hunter, the maid at Ashton Estates. Horrified
that she had fallen into bed with such a powerful man,
Lara fled the scene, leaving Eli wanting more. Could
he convince Lara that their estate affair was the stuff
fairy tales were made of?

Available at your favorite retail outlet.

Silhouette® Desire®

presents the next book in

Maureen Child's

miniseries

THREE WAY WAGER

*The Reilly triplets bet they could go
ninety days without sex. Hmm.*

WHATEVER REILLY WANTS...

(Silhouette Desire #1658)
Available June 2005

All Connor Reilly had to do to win his no-sex-
for-ninety days bet was spend time with the
one woman who wouldn't tempt him. Yet
Emma Jacobsen had other plans, plans that
involved a *very* short skirt and a change
in attitude. Emma's transformation had
Connor forgetting about his wager—but
was what they had strong enough to last
more than ninety days?

Available at your favorite retail outlet.